DOMINION FIRST BLOOD

Series Book Three

CAIUS

RICHARD MANN

"Fabulous book! Science thriller with a feel of history. It pulled me from the first page. Plenty of action, adventure and unusual twists. The characters are masterly written and author's attention to details deserves a lot of praise. At times I felt like I was traveling in time and space and it reminds me Star Wars and Lord of the Rings. Highly recommend this book to all Sci-fi lovers. Looking forward to your next book Richard Mann!"

By Iryna Dudinaon 25 November 2017 | Verified Purchase

 "An outstanding piece of work. Destined to be a classic. It's the best action adventure book I've read in years, gripping,edge of seat excitement, a real page turner. It's a mix of sci-fi action thriller horror and historical fiction...Frederick Forsyth and Bernard Cromwell on steroids..
This is quite a long book..but it needs to be. There is real depth on the characters..they feel alive and real. I really love Cockney Vinnie the sexy femme fatale vampire lucia and the flawed complex hero Bullet Proof Pete. I felt I could relate to the characters. There are many funny moments (esp. When 2 tough SAS heroes dress up as women).
     There's also an interesting love triangle but I won't go into it here as it will spoil the story. There is plenty of fascinating backstory....WWII and Roman times.i felt like I was there..i like the old fashioned chapter titles pictures appendices and history. Can't wait for book two."

By Dan 8 November 2017 Format: Paperback | Verified Purchase

"A tried and tested formula, aliens invade earth destroying and enslaving humanity. But this has an unusual twist. Humanity fights back with vampires as allies. A well-written book that will have you hooked from the first to the last page. It's reminiscent of Lord of the Rings in scope and adventure. Can't wait for the sequel."

By Celine 16 September 2017 Format: Kindle Edition | Verified Purchase

"Excellent effort by a new author!
Full of ambition and wide-ranging scope.
Something for lovers of Sci-Fi, action heroes and with vampires thrown in for good measure!"

By DejiDeal 15 September 2017 Format: Kindle Edition | Verified Purchase

"Although I'm not a big reader this book was very easy to read which kept pulling me closer and closer. The characters were very interesting and the plot twists and surprises kept the reader engrossed in the story, it's clear to see the author has put a lot of effort into the research that's gone into this book.
     The quality of the book itself is also very good, however you wouldn't expect less for the price. This book has definitely peaked my interest in reading more books and I can't wait for the sequel."
By David on 5 September 2017 Format: Paperback | Verified Purchase

"What a vivid imagination the author must have. The story is so well laid out one has virtually to be arrested to put the book down. I will not go into the story here except to say that it covers the globe and ventures into space. I'm looking forward to book 2. Don't be long Richard mann." By Chris 22 August 2017 Format: Kindle Edition | Verified Purchase

Give feedback on the book email: richardgmann@yahoo.co.uk

Follow me on Twitter: @richardgmann

Follow me and Like my Facebook Page: facebook.com/richardgmann.author

Facebook Group: Richard Mann Author Sci-Fi Group

Sign up on my website for my newsletter for book updates, new book releases, stories behind the books, competitions, news, and gossip. You can easily signup by entering your name and email

First edition

This book is dedicated to my family
who are the rock of my life. To
my mother Patricia you have always been there for us.

"Sometimes doing your best is not good enough.
Sometimes you must do what is required."

Sir Winston Churchill

"A time to love, and a time to hate, a
time of war, and a time of peace."

Ecclesiastes 3:8

CONTENTS

CAST OF CHARACTERS

Captain Peter 'Bulletproof' Morgan - SAS soldier / MI6 agent

Corporal Vinnie 'The Terminator' Carson - SAS soldier

Lucia - Vampire Elder and member of the Vampiri Grand Council

Count Cassian - Vampire Elder and Head of the Vampiri Grand Council

Jennifer Morgan – Peter's wife

Frank Wilson - US President

General Bill Scott - US Chief of Defense Staff

General Julian Grimbald - Head of US Space command

Professor Picard – Eccentric French Polymath

Father Sebastian Harris - Priest. Ex SAS

Sir Nigel Goldbroom – MI6 Chief

Ergtuk the 82nd – Sumeri Alien Clone

Herr Herg-Zuk – Sumeri Alien Emperor

Marshall Zurg-Uk – Sumeri Alien Defense Chief

Lord Grim-Uk – Sumeri Alien Narzuk SS Chief

Himm-Uk – Sumeri Alien Narzuk SS Deputy Chief

Gill Carson – Vinnie's wife

'Handsome' Mike - US Navy Seal

General Mike Schmitt – Sirius Defense Chief

Captain Duke Miller – CIA agent

Colonel Bradley – 21 regiment SAS Colonel

Colonel Stan Wight – Sirius base Colonel

Please note: The Appendices: Afterword, Cockney Slang table and Vampiri and Sumeri Alien command structure are at the back of the book.

"I imagine they might exist in massive ships, having used up all the resources from their home planet. Such advanced aliens would perhaps become nomads, looking to conquer and colonize whatever planets they can reach."

"To my mathematical brain, the numbers alone make thinking about aliens perfectly rational."

"The real challenge is working out what aliens might actually be like." "We only have to look at ourselves to see how intelligent life might develop into something we wouldn't want to meet."

"If aliens ever visit us, I think the outcome would be much as when Christopher Columbus first landed in America, which didn't turn out very well for the American Indians."

Professor Stephen Hawking

CAIUS

CHAPTER 1

PICARD SPILLS THE BEANS

A device beeps on the professor's wrist. 'Peter, Lucia follow me!' as he rushes off to his laboratory. He barges into his lab and checks his computer terminal: it is making a beeping sound. A button is flashing red.

'Sacre bleu!' mutters the professor. He is joined by Lucia and Peter. The professor is muttering to himself as he looks at the screen. Lucia and Peter sit down and look at the professor.

'Is there something you need to tell us, Professor?' Lucia asks. She knows he is hiding something.

'Your visions have been getting worse, haven't they Peter?' she asks, looking at her lover.

'I cannot hide anything from you, Lucia,' replies Peter wiping his brow, knowing that she hears his tortured mutterings during his sleep. She often comes to his room, to sleep with him, and comfort him. It seems normal now.

The professor clears his throat, avoiding their gaze.

'I have been analyzing the movements of the mothership. I have been looking for something specific. Very specific. The mothership has ejected one of its sections, and it has fallen to the Earth. Italy to be precise. Sicily. Mount Etna.'

'There is something in that section Professor, I can feel it,' says Lucia.

'The thing from my dreams,' adds Peter. Lucia touches his hand, feeling his pain. 'What have you not been telling us, Professor?' Peter is searching for the answer to his dreams.

'I am sorry young Peter. I did not tell you before, you have so much on your shoulders already.'

Peter stands up, his deep voice booming. 'What is it Professor? Tell me!'

The professor clears his throat again. 'You must complete one final test, Peter, before you become Caius. I have read the Book of

Borossus from start to finish. It is very clear on this.'

'What test?' asks Peter now sitting down.

'There is an ancient creature. An ancient demon who lives in the depths of the mountains of the Sumeri home planet, Ergal 5.'

'Why didn't you mention this before Professor?

'I am sorry mon ami I…I didn't want to alarm you. They have brought it onto their ship. I have been tracking it.'

'It is a demon,' says Peter. 'No wonder I haven't been sleeping lately.'

'Oui, my boy, and not a nice demon,' replies the professor.

'There are good and bad demons?' asks Peter.

'Yes Peter, I am a good demon,' Lucia winks at Peter. Peter leans across to the professor ignoring his vampire lover.

'I can feel like it…it speaks to me in my dreams. It frightens me, I don't mind telling you. Tell me more Professor,' replies Peter.

'His name is Bael. He is the first of the 72 spirits of Solomon that he used to build his temple with. Bael has 66 legions of hell at his disposal. He is equal in rank to the Archangel Raphael, so very powerful.'

'But less powerful than the Archangel Michael, my patron?' adds Peter.

'Correct, but even Michael would be wary of Bael. He is a king of Hell and can take many shapes or forms, including a toad or a human. He is very cunning and clever, beware if he speaks to you.'

'He is known to me,' says Lucia.

'The Sumeri are fools if they think they can control it. It will use them for its own evil ends, mark my words,' sighs the professor.

'That demon will not share power with da filthy Sumeri. It is a deceiver,' hissed Lucia, showing her fangs.

'Remember Peter, demons were once God's angels, and so they can make themselves look beautiful and claim to have more knowledge than they really do, but ultimately they only want to cause chaos and misery.'

'It seems to be the opposite of me,' sighs Peter.

'It is the anti-hero. You're the opposite Peter. To become Caius, you must defeat it. And you must do it alone.'

'Ok. I will get hold of Kojak. We leave for Sicily tonight,' says Peter with a grim but resolute look on his face.

'I'm coming with you,' insists Lucia.

'I will tell the general. He will not be pleased,' adds Professor Picard scratching his beard.

'I have more things to worry about than grumpy generals Professor.'

'Oui. You must stop it, Peter—else it wreaks havoc to all our ruin!'

CHAPTER 2

THE MOUNTAIN OF FIRE

Peter looked behind him as he climbed Mount Etna on a beautiful Mediterranean day. The sun shone bright above with hardly a cloud in the sky. Kojak was outside the X-37D sitting on the volcanic soil having a cigarette. He waved to Peter, who wore standard-issue army desert fatigues but had no weapons, apart from his PR1 sidearm, and his hunting knife on his side.

He had no need—not where he was going.

Peter looked at Lucia as she walked beside him. Loyal to a fault, but he felt bad about leaving Vinnie behind. Back at the base, there had been a heated argument with Vinnie who felt offended that he was going without him, but when he explained to his old friend what he had to do, he understood.

He felt the sun on his cheek as they climbed up the slope. Then he heard a shout behind him. Vinnie came running up the slope and stopped beside them.

'In for a penny, in for a pound,' Vinnie smiled.

Peter understood now. He could never leave his best friend behind.

'I hid in the storage area,' grinned Vinnie, then added, 'General Scott wants your guts for garters by the way.'

They both laughed then Peter became serious.

'Vinnie, I have a demon to conquer. I need to find my inner energy.'

They walked up the slope in silence, through volcanic ash and boulders. Up ahead they could see a steam vent, and they could smell the whiff of sulphur dioxide. On the other side of the mountain, they could see the massive wreck of a section of the alien mothership. An alien ship on an alien landscape. Peter thought it looked surreal. Like something from Dante's Inferno.

'That's where it crashed. The entity must be nearby.'

'As if we don't have enough to deal with—aliens, and now a fucking demon,' Vinnie coughed as he spoke. Then he had a coughing fit.

'Picard said a cave halfway up the mountain near an abandoned stone hut.' Peter checked his GPS, wiped his brow from the heat, then veered right. They climbed further up, and the smell of sulphur dioxide became worse. Vinnie started to struggle, and his breathing became laboured, Peter remembered he suffered from asthma in his childhood.

Up ahead, about a quarter of a mile they could see a cave, nearby was a volcanic vent with steam gushing from it.

'He is near,' said Lucia eyes looking straight ahead, her body rigid, like she had seen a ghost.

'I can feel his presence,' Peter replied. Then he looked at Lucia and remembered when she had seen the nun—she had the same expression.

'Lucia, you cannot help me. I must do this alone.'

'I know. May the Gods go with you,' and she kissed him. Peter looked at Vinnie who was having breathing difficulties. 'Lucia, stay here and look after Vinnie.' Then he turned and strode up to the cave.

Alone.

It was bigger now, bigger than it had looked before. He could hear noises inside of it. He swigged some water and strode in, stopping at the entrance, trying to get a feel for the place, and letting his intuition take over.

Behind him was the daylight. Before him a dark, forbidding cave, 20 feet high and 50 feet wide.

As he walked in out of the light and into semi-darkness, he could hear a rumble deep below the volcano as if it was erupting. As he walked further into the cave's darkness, it now seemed strangely quiet. On his right now, about a hundred feet away he could see a stream of red-hot orange lava flowing like a river.

As he got nearer to it, he could feel the heat from it. Then he saw something out of the corner of his eye.

A movement.

CHAPTER 3

THE MAKING OF CAIUS: BATTLE OF THE GODS

Now, in front of him, where once there was no one, is a figure, a shining figure, in golden robes, with long golden hair and blue eyes. The entity is smiling at him and is surrounded by a golden light. Peter stepped forward one step, like a moth drawn to the light.

The entity opened its arms to him in a welcoming gesture.

'Caius, that is your name, is it not?' asked the entity, its blue eyes shining, is voice like golden honey.

'Yes, I am Caius. I was not expecting this,' he replied, but he took another step forward. His mother's words rang in his ears: '*All that glitters is not gold.*' A shiver went up his spine as he became entranced by the beautiful blue eyes of the demon in front of him.

'I am Bael. I am powerful, I can help you. There is no need for us to fight, Caius,' Bael said reasonably, 'for I know what you are—the Eternal Warrior. Your patron will not make you powerful, Caius. You will be his slave,' a vindictive tone was in his voice, his eyes taking on a red hue.

Peter then remembered the last words of the professor, '*Do not let him speak else he will charm you, and you shall perish!*'

'Come join me. We will rule the Earth together, with me and my legions we will be kings on Earth.' Bael opened his arms to Peter. 'I can satisfy your every whim, every desire; your lust for the beautiful demon, Lucia, is legendary, is it not, Caius? I can see it!' Bael blinked, and a second later another entity appeared: a woman, but not a woman.

'Caius, I am Lilith, I have looked upon you from afar.' Caius was entranced by her beauty. She exuded animal magnetism as her long tongue licked her lips, her eyes were wells of desire. Pure lust. 'I desire you, a man of strength and power,' she said in a husky voice. Then Lilith looked at him, and his desire raged, for she was indeed beautiful. Dark brown eyes, long black hair, full red lips, full naked breasts, and rounded hips. A long black snake curled up her legs, hissed and then entered her, and she gasped and moaned and writhed with pleasure. Her chest moved up and down as her jewelled hands rubbed her breasts and nipples, her eyes rolling in desire. Peter moved his foot forward again.

'Caius, Caius come to me. I want you, take me…'

He remembered the legends of Lilith, the demon who would visit young men in their dreams and steal their souls, but his lust rose as he gazed at her; he tried to stop himself.

'Caius, together we can be lovers. I want you, Caius, we can be gods together!'

Lilith's breasts heaved up and down with desire. He stopped his legs moving forward; *he would soon be lost.* He remembered the four words etched in silver flames on his sword. He had to break the spell before it was too late and he was overwhelmed by desire!

'Michael!' Lilith and Bael screamed at the name. 'Saday! Athanatos! Sabaoth!' Peter broke free from the spell and fell to his knees breathing heavily in the warm, volcanic atmosphere.

Lilith screamed again and disappeared.

Bael bellowed with rage as his appearance changed to his true self, Bael, a king of Hell. Flames leaped around the demon as he transformed. He now had the head of a green toad, and two horns sprung from his head, his two red eyes glowered at Caius in rage, a black forked tongue slithered in and out of his mouth. His body was that of a giant hairy man as flames leapt around him. 'Your cause is hopeless Caius. You will not find your Jennifer. She is lost!'

Peter was now hit by a stench so foul he choked and then staggered in the hot cave facing the true face of the demon, Bael. He had to destroy him before it was too late. He had to find the strength. He could not wither before the terrible entity that faced him.

His mind entered an altered state: the Eternal Warrior. He clenched a handful of volcanic sand in the cave and rubbed it into his hands. Time itself seemed to stop, the evil entity still, frozen. Caius had a vision of a sword, a large silver sword, with a golden pommel and jewels, amethysts, embedded into the pommel.

'Caliburnus!'   'Caliburnus!'   'Caliburnus!'

Three times he said the words of power as he closed his eyes, focusing on the sword in his mind, and when he opened them, he was holding it in his hand. It felt powerful and vibrated with enormous power, as the silver blade gave off a light. All around him was a blue light. Lightning sprang from the blade striking Bael, who staggered backward, his chest smoking from the strike. The four holy words etched on the sword blazed with a silver light; the dragon emblem was alive with silver fire.

Bael now had a look of fear on his ugly toad face, his black forked tongue slithering in and out of its mouth. His body was now that of a black bear as he shape-shifted trying to gain an advantage. Caius stepped forward with his sword, but Bael now had a trident in his hand and stood fast. A deep growl came from deep within the demon.

'Your puny sword is no match for my trident, human, it was forged in the pits of hell. It cannot be broken!'

'I am Caius. My patron is the Archangel Michael himself. And this is his sword!' Caius brought his sword up high above his head, his sinewy arm muscles tightened and brought down the mighty sword onto Bael, who brought up his trident just in time There was an almighty clash of steel as the sword hit the trident, breaking one of the three forks. Lightning flashed from the sword, hitting Bael in the chest.

'Your puny trident is no match for my holy sword. It is one of the seven holy swords of the Archangel Michael. The one who cast you and your serpent master from Heaven. Michael, the one who stands before the throne of God himself!' Caius's voice boomed in the cave.

A look of fear and sadness came over Bael's toad face. He hesitated, as he relived the experience of being ejected from Heaven, and gave Caius the split second he needed. He brought his sword down on Bael's leg, slicing it off at the knee. Bael fell onto his back, screaming blasphemies at Caius.

'Curse you and your kind!'

Caius stepped forward and sliced the toad head clean off Bael, but the toady eyes still blinked as the head lay on the floor of the cave.

'I return to my master, Caius, but we will meet again.' The eyes looked sad and then closed. His patron Michael then appeared in glorious light and offered him a golden cup. Caius took the cup and drank the crystal cool liquid. He felt the energy in him being renewed. There was a look of pride in the archangel's eyes—then his patron was gone.

Caius's appearance changed. He was taller, his muscles were more solid, he felt like he had the strength of 20 men. His eyes blazed a deeper blue, and his voice deepened.

'I am Caius,' he said in a loud booming voice which echoed around the cave.

Something changed inside him then. The balance had been tipped, he was no longer Peter. He was now Caius, ancient warrior, returned to save mankind, and nothing, not a flaming demon, green-skinned aliens or a trumped up, pompous general, was going to get in his way. The warrior blood rushed through his veins, the strength of 20 men – 20 warriors.

The transformation to Caius was now complete.

As he stood there, Lucia came quietly up behind him and looked at the decapitated head of the defeated demon. 'You won!' she said as she looked at him and understood. 'You are no longer Peter. You possess the look of a demi-god. No one can stop you now.'

'Lucia, I am now Caius,' a tear fell down his cheek and she went on tiptoes to kiss him on the lips. Then his sword and Bael the demon vanished. As they walked out of the cave into the sunshine, Caius took a swig of water and held Lucia in his arms.

'I passed the test. He offered me the kingdoms of the world, Lucia. Even to have my desires satiated by a demon—Lilith. But I said no.' Lucia smiled, 'Empty promises my love, besides I want you for myself. You can only have one demon lover.'

'Lucia, previously the world around me dictated my actions, now I have awakened and become the person I was destined to be. Now I will shape, and change the world around me. I am Caius.'

'You were meant to fight that demon, Caius, I am proud of you.'

Vinnie was now in a bad way as they carried him down the slope of the volcano back to the X-37D. 'Kojak, get the medical kit, we need oxygen quick!' shouted Caius. Kojak retrieved an oxygen bottle; Caius put the mask on Vinnie's mouth and made sure it was secure. Vinnie looked pale and disorientated. Kojak looked at Caius, a look of wonder on his face. 'You have changed, laddy.'

'I am Caius now. My former self is gone forever.'

'I'm still going to call you Pete,' whispered Vinnie. Caius smiled. Lucia's mind crossed time and space as she contacted her master. 'He has defeated the demon Bael. The prophecy is fulfilled. His transformation to Caius is now complete.'

CHAPTER 4

THE BOOK OF BOROSSUS

In the grim, silent, cold darkness of the secret vampire lair in the Blue Ridge mountains, Lady Vesilia was asleep in a dark green gown. Her long hair flowed on either side of her as she lay on the large four poster bed in a cave. Suddenly her eyes opened then she leaped from her bed.

She opened the wooden door and ran to the hidden entrance of the mountain lair, a large steel door covered in rock. From the outside, it was just a mountainside. She shapeshifted to squeeze through a small fissure in the stone, just four inches wide, until she stood on a rock ledge on the mountainside, the hidden entrance now behind her.

A large blue moon shone above her. Then she saw it: a black shape moving through the darkness—an alien ship!

She shapeshifted back into the lair and raised the alarm. A siren sounded as vampires of various clans donned their leather armour and swords. Baron Titas, old and wizened, wearing a leather jerkin, ran towards her. 'Baron, the alien filth have found us! Defend the entrance at all costs. I must protect the book!'

'I will make them pay in blood!' cried Baron Titus, retrieving his sword, and sliding daggers into leather scabbards on his boots and thigh.

Vampire warriors gathered around the Baron wielding swords, as Vesilia ran at lightning speed across the stone floor to a room at the back of the network of caves and caverns. She lifted a large key from a belt around her waist and opened the steel door. She went inside, then locked it again. She looked at the large wooden chest which contained the ancient book. Ancient runes were carved on the chest, special runes cast by Cassian to protect the book. Whoever opened the chest and tried to remove the book without removing the protection spell would get a nasty surprise, but only Cassian could remove the spell with a golden key, and he had given her the key, but she could not find it! In all the chaos she had mislaid it. Still, at least no-one would be able to steal the book. It was safe.

Vesilia shivered as she hears a loud boom: they were pounding the outer door. It was one foot thick—surely not? Then a louder boom and a crack. Vesilia knew they had got through the door. Then there were shouts, the loud shrieking voice of Baron Titas, sounds of laser blasters, shrieks, and the yells of vampires in the heat of battle.

Then silence.

Then the guttural sounds of alien voices outside the door. Vesilia drew her long runed sword from its scabbard holding it in both hands.

'Come and taste the steel of my sword you filthy scum!' she shouted, her warrior blood rising, her eyes flashing red. There was an explosion as the door exploded inwards knocking her onto the floor. She got up dazed, coughing on the dust, but sword still raised. Through the smoke, she could see a shape, a black shape. Out of the shadows stepped a figure all in black, wearing a thin smile, haughty and empty-eyed, like he had no soul. A wiry Sumeri alien was wearing a thin smile; laser blaster in hand, and an evil glint in his red tainted eyes.

'I am Lord Grim-Uk of the Imperial Sumeri army.'

'Begone you filth!' screamed Vesilia.

'Night-Crawler, you have something I desire. You will give it to me!'

'Whatever it is you want, it is not here!' Vesilia wiped the dust from her eyes, showing her fangs, her eyes blazing a deeper red. She watched as the smiling alien put a pill into his mouth. His demeanour changed: his eyes were now red, and he started fidgeting. The Narzuk SS Stormtroopers rushed at her as she fought like a demon, killing two with one thrust of her sword, then another. Then Grim-Uk fired his blaster, and she staggered and fell, wounded in her chest.

'You will give it to me!' Then Vesilia changed her tone. 'It is here in that box. Take it.'

'I do not trust you.' Grim-Uk beckoned to one of his Narzuk SS troopers and pointed at the box. The trooper stood back, looking at the runes which now glowed like fire on the box, then looked at Grim-Uk, fear in his eyes.

Grim-Uk pushed the reluctant soldier forward. 'Open it—that's an order!'

'Alien filth, you will regret opening Pandora's box!'

The trooper blasted the metal padlock with his laser blaster then opened the large wooden lid of the box. Grim-Uk stepped back a pace. Then the soldier reached his hand inside the box to pick up the book.

Suddenly golden flames shot out of the box and enveloped the soldier, who burst into flames, shouting and screaming in pain, as he collapsed into a burning heap onto the floor, the stink of burning flesh filling the room.

Then Grim-Uk pushed another trooper forward, and as he put his hand in the wooden box, he also erupted into golden flames.

'You take the book!' shouted Grim-Uk to the injured Vesilia.

'Never, you alien filth!' she replied as she spat and showed her fangs.

Then two troopers brought a bloody Baron Titas to Grim-Uk.

'Give me the book or I kill him!'

'Vesilia, don't do it!' screamed Baron Titas.

Vesilia saw a ventilation duct in the corner of the room. She moved like lightning, grabbed the thick book from the box as golden flames went up here arms burning her, and went to jump up to the corner of the room, but she was not quick enough. As she jumped she felt the heat of a laser blast on her back, and she fell to the ground unconscious, her back and arms burnt.

'Search her for the key!' ordered Grim-Uk.

They found a key in a secret pocket in her dress. A golden key.

Grim-Uk inserted the key into the book, then took the book from her hands then nodded to his Stormtroopers. They shot the Baron, then used his own sword to slice his head off, then left, walking over their dead comrades. 'We have paid the price in blood for this book,' said Grim-Uk.

'I have failed you, Cassian, my love,' Vesilia cried as she lay injured on the stone floor. She summoned her last energy to contact Cassian. "My love, the filth has invaded our sanctuary. They have taken the sacred book of power. They have taken the Book of Borossus!" she wept. But she could not contact him, for she was too weak.

As Grim-Uk climbed aboard the hovering alien craft, he caressed the book in his arms, like a lover. 'The Emperor will be pleased,' he smiled as he boarded the jet-black alien craft. 'Comrades, let us give thanks to our God, almighty Bael,' he said, as he looked at the gathering before him. 'Praise be to Bael,' chanted his fellow Narzuk SS as they touched the black figurines around their necks. He raised the old magical tome above his head to show his loyal troops. 'Now we have occult power, we will rule the Earth!'

CHAPTER 5

ACHILLES HEEL

Lucia stopped in her tracks, standing rigid as a post. Her eyes distant—communicating, whispering incoherently in some ancient tongue. Peter and Vinnie looked at her.

'What is it, Lucia?' Caius touched her arm.

'I must find Cassian and the professor.' Lucia looked at Caius with a worried look on her face, then she ran off, a lightning blur, to find her master.

In a small conference room in the Mojave base sat Cassian, Professor Picard looking like he had aged ten years, and Lady Vesilia, looking dishevelled, bloody and frightened.

'Lady Vesilia, what happened?' asked Lucia.

'Lucia sit down,' ordered Cassian.

'I am so sorry Cassian…' Lady Vesilia's voice broke.

'Start from the beginning,' prompted Cassian gently.

'Our base in the mountains was overrun, we were taken by surprise. Baron Titas was lost…the others escaped. But…'

'But what?' asked Cassian.

'They took the book, the Book of Borossus.'

Cassian looked aghast while the professor put his head in the hands. 'I have failed you Cassian,' Lady Vesilia said, tears pouring from her eyes. Cassian passed her a handkerchief.

'You are burned,' said Lucia. 'The book, I did not remove the charm,' replied a sad Vesilia.

'Who took it?' asked Cassian patiently.

'It was Grim-Uk. Vlad-Uk's acolyte.'

'He is known to me. Many friends of mine were taken on the orders of Vlad-Uk over the centuries. The vendetta still lives,' replied Cassian, his tone ice cold. Then he added, 'They desire the magical power in the book, they want its secrets.'

'It's worse than you think,' said the professor slowly. 'There is an incantation in the book, which can rob Caius of his powers if they find the passage.'

'Then we are lost,' spoke Cassian solemnly.

'How do I recognize him, so I can kill him?' asked Lucia.

'He has red veins running through his eyes, a result of being addicted to their fertility and drug boosters. He is a drug addict and unpredictable—be careful.'

'Lucia, he is the embodiment of evil,' added Vesilia. 'Even though we are demons, we still live by laws. He has offended us and must be punished. Kill Grim-Uk for Baron Titus.'

Lucia nodded. 'It will be my pleasure.'

'We will both kill him,' said Cassian. 'If we get the chance.'

Cassian touched a tearful Vesilia's arm. 'Vesilia, my love. Go rest. Leave us.' Cassian gave one of his rare smiles as she left—a promise that he would see her later. She half smiled at him as she closed the door behind her.

'What is this Achilles heel, Professor?' as Cassian regarded his old friend.

'It is an obscure passage near the end of the book, I suspect it would be difficult for the filthy aliens to translate. It is a one-line incantation in ancient Greek, which robs Caius of his powers—only temporarily, but it might be enough for them to kill him.'

'Caius must not know,' said Lucia solemnly.

'Lucia is correct. If he finds out it might affect the outcome of our mission,' replied the professor, scratching his beard.

'Why?' asks Cassian.

'Any doubt in Caius's mind may affect the outcome—quantum mechanics, Cassian. Schrödinger's cat. Observation of the event can affect the outcome. He must not know!' The professor banged his fist on the table.

'Cassian, you say Vlad-Uk has lived for centuries—highly unusual for a failing race. Did he make a pact?' asked the professor putting two and two together.

'Yes he made a pact with Bael himself, hence his unnaturally long life. He is cursed, like us.'

'It is no wonder God has turned his back on them,' sighed Lucia.

CHAPTER 6

ALIEN HEALING

Caius and Lucia walked down the corridor to the medical centre – Lucia looked at Caius, worried about his achilles heel, but he looked like a god now, surely nothing could stop him. They found President Wilson, who was on his deathbed. Michael, his son, was with him, holding his father's hand. As the president tried to rise from his bed, Michael was crying.

President Wilson smiled weakly as he saw Caius through blurry eyes; his appearance had changed. And a red-faced Scott had been looking for him too.

'Hello son, best get that priest friend of yours, I think I'm dying.'

'Don't you worry sir, you will be up and chasing nurses in no time.'

'You look different son,' said the president as Caius retrieved the alien medical device from his rucksack and gave it to Lucia. She pressed some buttons, and it started humming. She ran it over the body of the president, the light penetrating his organs, back and forth, back and forth. President Wilson suddenly took in a large lungful of air and fell unconscious. Michael burst into tears, looking at Caius and Lucia, pleading.

'Is Daddy alive?'

Lucia examined the president. 'I think so. He is old, so he will take some time to recover.' Caius looked at the president, he was fond of him, wise, like a father figure. He crossed himself and prayed to his patron Michael, touching the sigil on his arm. He had the impression of a loving presence by his side, as he prayed.

'Your daddy will be fine,' smiled Caius at Michael, hoping he was right.

'I'm hoping that device did the trick,' Caius said as he comforted the boy, looking at Lucia.

A big, burly and very strict-looking nurse walked in with a face that could turn milk sour. Hands on hips she barked at them.

'What did you do to him?'

'Saved his life, I hope,' said Lucia.

'You two get out of here, now!'

Michael looked up at Caius with big wet eyes.

'Will Daddy be OK?'

'Don't worry, my friend Lucia said your father will get better.'

Caius looked at Lucia. 'Let's get some rest, there's nothing else we can do now,' he said as they walked out the room into the corridor. Lucia smiled at Caius, got on tiptoes, and kissed him on the cheek. She looks as though she was in two minds about this human man.

Was it possible for a vampire to feel love?

What did her heart tell her?

Could she be mortal? Could his patron help her?

Could Caius help her become human again?

She cleared her mind, removing all emotional clutter, as she triggered her clairvoyant powers and analyzed all the possible pathways. She remembered all that her Uncle Louis had taught her how to be a human computer. Analyze all threads, probable choices, probable outcomes, dependencies of decisions.

What were the weak points, and the strong points? There were other powers at work here as well.

The nun. She thought back to the nun. Was it a message? Could she be human again? Everything was coming to a head. Very soon, all would be resolved one way or the other. We either live, or we die, and Caius was the one key for all paths.

Caius.

She looked at him again.

'Me and Uncle Louis need to interrogate Ergtuk first. Join us.'

CHAPTER 7

ALIEN INTERROGATION

Lucia and Caius walked into a sealed room. The professor was waiting,

'Hello Professor, it's good to see you again.'

Picard stared, then smiled in wonder at Caius. 'You conquered the demon, the transformation is complete, mon ami.' He was taller, his muscles were more solid, his eyes blazed a deeper blue, and his voice had deepened. He looked as though he had the strength of 2 men.

'You look like an ancient Greek god, Caius,' the professor added. Lucia smiled in admiration at her handsome Greek god, the lust rising in her belly. 'It is the prophecy,' she said as she ran her hands over his chest.

There were several pieces of equipment in the room, none of which looked pleasant. Two nervous armed guards hovered near Ergtuk, who is strapped to a chair and could not move. Strong lights blinded the alien clone, who looked upset and disorientated.

The professor looked at Ergtuk in silence for a minute, and then turned to Caius and Lucia.

'What is your measure of him, mon ami?

'Do not trust him, he is a filthy alien, one of those Sumeri!' said Lucia through gritted teeth, her eyes a pale shade of red. Caius shook his head.

'Hold on a moment. I think he genuinely wants to help us. Listen, professor, by what I can make out Ergtuk needs our help, he does not have long to live. As you know, these aliens are a failing race. Ergtuk told me the aliens have two races. The ruling elite—the Narzuks (the military), along with the Patricians, and the Grays, who are the slave clones. Due to genetic deterioration, the Narzuks and Patricians have cloned versions of themselves over thousands of years. Ergtuk here has only a few years. If we help him, he will help us.'

'I think maybe there is a way we can help him. I wrote a paper on DNA cloning a few years ago. I have some theories on genetic decay,' added the professor.

'What's the problem with Ergtuk? Why are the clones dying?' asked Peter.

'Replicant fading. Each time you clone you're making a copy of a copy. Subtle errors creep into the chromosomes. Each iteration is a weaker version and has a shorter lifespan. Eventually, you end up with an unviable clone,' replied Picard in a matter-of-fact tone.

Ergtuk seemed nervous as he looked at the armed guards, who were pointing a rifle at him. 'Please leave the room,' Caius asked the guards.

'We are under strict instructions from General Scott himself not to leave the alien alone,' they replied.

'I will be responsible for him, just wait outside the door. I will shout if there's a problem, thanks.'

The guards went reluctantly out of the room as Lucia shook her head. Ergtuk looked at Caius and smiled thanks in his eyes. Professor Picard gestured to Caius to continue. The professor had wanted himself and Lucia to do the interrogation, but despite the language difficulties, and to his surprise, this young Caius had made a connection with the alien.

'Peter—sorry, Caius, before I forget, this prototype device will translate what Ergtuk is saying.' Professor Picard attached a headphone device that plugged into Caius's ear and a microphone. 'It contains the known vocabulary of the aliens, though these Gray clones may have a different dialect.'

'Ergtuk, are you okay? Would you like some water?' Ergtuk nodded, and Caius gave him some water, but did not undo his straps. Caius moved the spotlights away, and Ergtuk nodded.

'Do we really need these straps?' Caius looked across at the professor. The professor shrugged while Lucia shook her head in anger. Caius undid the straps as Lucia drew her sword in the blink of an eye and held the blade to Ergtuk's throat. Her diatribe in alien could not be mistaken, and Ergtuk looked frightened and shrunk away.

'If you are quite finished, Lucia,' Caius glared at his vampire lover as she put her sword away, his blue eyes blazing.

Caius went to speak into the translation mouthpiece that the professor had given him. Ergtuk looked puzzled, but then Caius adjusted it, and he smiled.

'Why do you want to join us Ergtuk?' Caius was curious as to his motivation, looking for certain signs.

'I had a friend. This is very unusual for a clone. His name was Argvorn the twenty-first. We used to talk about things. We were training to be soldiers. I did not want to be a soldier. We had learned about the Earth, and I thought it looked incredible. Why would our masters want to desecrate this beautiful planet and enslave its people? We did not like this. We thought it was wrong. We had so many questions. Why did the Patricians live in luxury while the Plebeians lived in the polluted hovels? What would it be like to have a family? What would sex be like? We laughed at that. We were different— clones are not supposed to laugh. We were caught once laughing, and I was put into a detention cell for a month, for *"re-education."* I experienced a feeling, I think you call it *"resentment."* We used to eat together. One-day Argvorn asked a question of a Narzuk training officer who walked by our table, 'Why are we invading the human planet, what have they done? The next day he was gone. When I asked where he was, I found out he had been taken away for *"re-processing."* I never saw him again. Then I experienced another feeling, it was sadness. Then another, *anger.'*

'We need information about the command structure of the aliens. Who is in charge?' asked Caius.

The earpiece translated Ergtuk's reply.

'General Grimbald is nominally in charge, but the real leader is Marshal Zurg-Uk. Grimbald follows his orders. When the invasion is complete, they will sideline him. I have heard rumours that the marshal is not happy with Grimbald's progress.'

'Pawn in a bigger game,' muttered Caius.

'There is another: Lord Grim-Uk. He is head of the Narzuk SS unit, the ones who set up the resettlement camps and harvest the human women. They are evil, Caius. We are afraid of them, any of us who question orders are taken away.'

'The ones with the red armbands?'

'Yes. We live in a climate of fear, Caius. There are rumours that they worship a demon, they are most ungodlike. They have a secret cult.' Ergtuk gazed at the mighty warrior hoping he would be his saviour.

'I know, I met the demon,' replied Caius recalling the experience. He was in the cave again, sweat dripping from his body, sword in hand facing the demon Bael, its black tongue moving in and out of his mouth. Then he struck and he had conquered his demon and it was over.

CHAPTER 8

QUID QUO PRO

Caius cleared his throat.

'We need information about the layout of the mothership, Ergtuk. Our wives are on board on that ship, we are almost certain of it.'

Ergtuk looked like an amateur poker player who possessed a winning hand. He remained silent for a moment. Lucia gave Caius a stern look as if he was giving away too much information, then Ergtuk spoke.

'If I give you this information, do you promise to give me sanctuary?'

'I promise,' said Caius.

'And find a way to help me live?' as he looked at the professor.

'Yes, I will do my best, there is hope for you, Ergtuk,' Professor Picard reassured him in his native dialect.

Ergtuk looked at all of them, and then looked at Caius and smiled. 'I work for Oluk, the chief engineer of the mothership. I like Oluk, he is nice to me. I trained to be a soldier, but I didn't like it, so I became a computer programmer instead. I am good at it, so my instructor agreed. There was a rush to get the mothership finished for the invasion. Oluk told me the ship was structurally unsound, and they were working round the clock to keep it going. I know for a fact the software systems are unstable as we were told to make shortcuts.'

The professor looked horrified. 'Sacre bleu! There are no shortcuts in computer programming. It's a bit like saying to a heart surgeon, "Can you hurry up and take shortcuts please, I'm in a hurry" The result will be disastrous. But it's to our advantage,' he smiled.

'The software also looks after the shields, which help to keep the ship intact,' added Ergtuk.

'We've had reports of chunks falling off the mothership,' said the professor.

'Maybe that's a weakness we can exploit,' said Caius.

Ergtuk shook his head, 'the shields are very strong. They stopped the nuclear attack on our ship in your city of Chicago.'

Ergtuk drank some water. 'I have seen the plans of the mothership and the modifications made. There are several points where the ship is weakest. They are in the plans.'

'Where are the plans?' said the professor.

'I have them safely hidden. I took great risks to get the information,' Ergtuk added.

'Where exactly?'

'I have studied Earth culture, and you have a saying: where the sun does not shine.'

Caius grinned. They turned their backs while Ergtuk retrieved the device, not without a certain amount of pain and curses. Caius washed the device in a water fountain.

'Professor, can we do anything with this?' Caius handed the now cleaned alien data storage device to the professor.

'Oui, the interface is the same as the comms device you found. I will be back in a moment.' The professor hurried off, somewhat sprightly for someone his age. Caius helped Ergtuk button up the trousers he had given him, as Ergtuk put a hand on his shoulder.

'Peter..'

'Ergtuk, I am now Caius.' Ergtuk nodded.

'What is it like to have a real mother and father?'

Caius is taken aback by the question and is silent for a while; it was a deep question, and he thought back to his mother—kind and loving, always baking cakes. Whenever he came home from school, he could smell the cakes as he walked in and he would run into the kitchen to greet her. She had a wonderful smile which would light up the room as he ate the chocolate cakes.

And his father was always off on an adventure somewhere with the army. He wasn't home much, but he was excited when he did come home with presents and stories. He remembered waiting at the window for him. His heart would start to beat faster as he saw him walking down the garden path in his army uniform and bags. He would run down the path to meet him and throw his arms around him. I need to be a better father, thought Caius, as he realized how little he was home with his family. He felt guilty about it, then turned to Ergtuk.

'Ergtuk, it is a part of what we are, as humans. We look up to our fathers for advice and guidance, and to our mothers for comfort and love. There are very strong bonds between parents and children, all our lives. It is always there, even after death, they live on in our memories. I still remember my dad in his army uniform, coming home on leave. He would give us presents and tell stories. It was the best time.' Vinnie strolled into the room, munching a large beef burger.

'What about brothers and sisters?' Ergtuk's face is a picture of wonder and curiosity.

'Yes, again, there is a strong link. I was always fighting with my sister Ruth, but we love each other very much.'

Lucia smiled.

'Vinnie, here is my best friend. He is like a brother to me,' Caius added. 'We have been on many adventures together.'

'I would like to be your brother,' said Ergtuk.

Caius was touched by this strange alien, who seemed very human; he liked him. He smiled and clapped him on the back, and then he noticed Vinnie and Lucia looking at him in silence, trying to assimilate the change in him.

'What is it?' asked Caius.

'We're just trying to get used to you mate,' said Vinnie munching his burger.

'You look like a god. Nothing can stop us now,' smiled Lucia – she would visit him that night.

CHAPTER 9

TEA CEREMONY

The professor came bustling into the room with a technician carrying a projection device. The technician set up the projector and the professor plugged in the alien memory device via an adaptor he had invented. A large three-dimensional image appeared of the alien mothership.

'Can we make the image bigger, Professor? It's a very large mothership, I want to see detail,' asked Caius.

Professor Picard adjusted the image, making it three times bigger, almost filling the room. Ergtuk walked around the image, studying it in silence, then stopped at a certain point, looking unsure. Then his face became brighter.

'Here on Level 4, are two power plants close to one another. In Sector 15. The structural integrity of the mothership here is at its weakest. I overheard Oluk discussing it with one of his engineers. If you put a bomb here, you can cripple the ship.' Caius looked at Professor Picard.

'What do you think, Professor?'

'Mmm, I need to study these schematics a while before I concur.'

An image of Jennifer leaped into his mind as he looked at Ergtuk. He was a professional soldier, and the mission was critical, but Jennifer meant everything to him, and that was more important.

'Ergtuk, we need to know where the women are being held.' Vinnie and Caius locked eyes on the alien clone.

'You mean the central breeding chamber?' Vinnie and Caius nodded furiously, adrenalin running, waiting for Ergtuk's answer. Ergtuk looked at the holographic projection again, then at Caius, and understood his anxiety.

'Caius, it is located on the same level, here. Level 4 central chamber, in the centre of the ship. Sector 16. You will need to use the internal transporters, the ship is 100 of your Earth miles wide. I hope you find what you are looking for.'

'Sector 16. Thank you Ergtuk,' said a grateful and smiling Caius.

'Cheers Ergtuk. Have some beefburger.' Vinnie gave Ergtuk some of his beef burger which Ergtuk took a small bite from.

'Beef burger. It is nice. Thank you, Vinnie, brother of Caius.'

Ergtuk fell silent, his head drooping. They had come to an impasse. The alien looked tired and unwilling to carry on. Caius's mouth was dry after all the talking. 'What we need is a cup of tea.'

'You are a man after my own heart,' the professor smiled at Caius and thought it was a stroke of genius. 'Oui, mon ami a cup of tea would be good. And le biscuits.'

Ergtuk looked puzzled. 'Caius, what is a cup of tea? The education booths didn't teach us that.'

'You drink, don't you?'

'Yes, we need water like all carbon-based life forms.'

'It is a drink, a hot drink made from the infusion of plant leaves.'

Ergtuk nodded.

'Ideally in a teapot—a china teapot,' Caius added.

'China?' Ergtuk frowned.

'A pot made of clay that has been baked in an oven.'

'Sounds complicated, but fascinating,' Ergtuk smiled.

Caius poked his head outside the door and talked to the guard.

'Can you get us a pot of tea please, in a china teapot if you have one?'

'What's a teapot?' asked the guard.

'Jesus,' Caius looked heavenwards.

'Vinnie, go with the guard will you?' Lucia looked bored.

'I will go too,' said the professor, looking serious.

Several minutes later, a frustrated looking Vinnie and the professor were in the kitchen with the guard.

'No mate, look, the water must be boiling so the tea can brew properly,' said a frustrated Vinnie.

'Sacre bleu, the pot should be warmed first, then the water, not hot, but boiling water. It must be poured at a certain height onto the tea. Thus.' The bewildered guard followed their instructions.

Vinnie knocked on the interrogation room door a while later, a meek-looking guard following behind him. Caius opened the door. Then the professor walked in, shaking his head. Vinnie put his hand on his shoulder.

'Bulletproof, old mate, when this war is over, can we teach these yanks how to make a decent cup of tea?' Caius laughed as he took the metal teapot and put it on a table.

'You look tired, Professor.'

'It was the most difficult lecture I ever had to give.' Then he smiled as Vinnie found some chocolate biscuits. 'Good, we have le biscuits.'

Ergtuk looked at Caius as he stirred the tea, the professor and Vinnie watched Caius. Ergtuk looked fascinated.

'Ergtuk, the tea must be brewed for the precise amount of time: too soon, and it's too hot and not brewed. Too long and the tea is warm and stewed.' The professor nodded and looked at Caius, gauging the moment.

Caius nodded. The moment is now. He poured the tea into a cup and added milk and one teaspoon of sugar and stirred. The professor smiled as Caius offered the cup to Ergtuk, who delicately held the cup and tasted the liquid. Lucia looked bored as they watched him, her eyes rolling.

'Sip the tea, it will be hot,' said Caius to his new friend.

Ergtuk put the cup to his lips and felt the warm, refreshing liquid go down his throat. It felt comforting, refreshing and delicious, all at the same time. The professor thought he could write a Ph.D. thesis on the expressions coming from Ergtuk's face.

'I like it. It is, how you say, refreshing, delicious,' Ergtuk smiled.

They all beamed with pleasure, except Lucia, who was at a computer making herself busy. 'If you have quite finished with your tea ceremony, we have a war to fight,' she said, crossing her arms like a schoolmistress.

Ergtuk spoke. 'You now have the access codes to gain access, but you need to find a way to get to the mothership. You will need to use stealth, otherwise, you will be detected. I do not want to see your Earth destroyed and raped by my masters, it is too beautiful for that. You people, you are nice to me. Caius, you are my brother.'

A tear fell from Ergtuk's face.

CHAPTER 10

CAIUS HAS A PLAN

Caius went back to his quarters exhausted and crashed onto his bed, fully clothed. He could not remember the last time he had slept, even he, the mighty Caius, had his limits. He was grateful to have his own quarters, as Vinnie snored a lot, apart from anything else. As he settled down, he thought about the interrogation of Ergtuk and was glad he did not have to use coercion. He liked Ergtuk, and he felt responsible for him now. He hoped the professor would be able to help the clone, and save him before his DNA deteriorated any further.

As he lay there open-eyed, thinking about his transformational experience in conquering the demon Bael. He was now what he was meant to be – he had crossed a threshold, and it felt good, he had no fear now, for that was in the past – he had conquered all his demons, he was now Caius, the demi god.

But he could not sleep, as he thought about a plan to get on the ship. At least he knew where the women were being held, and most importantly, where his wife was, thanks to Ergtuk. Somehow, he must get on that ship. He had been on many dangerous missions but nothing as dangerous as what he was planning. For a rare moment, he had butterflies in his stomach. Just as he was about to drift off, Lucia came in and lay down beside him. She kissed him with her red lips, and he looked into her deep blue eyes as they both fell into a deep sleep.

Peter's eyes became heavy as he drifted into sleep. He was in a garden surrounded by a stone wall. The sun shone down on the garden, where herbs and flowers grew. He was wearing a gold medallion around his neck, as well as a toga and sandals, having come from an important meeting with two senators. He smiled as his two children came running up to him. He played with them, then sniffed the rosemary. It would go with the lamb which their servants were cooking. Their new servant girl, strolled into the garden, along the path, and smiled shyly at him, her long brown hair blowing in the soft breeze as she walked past him. She bowed, and walked towards their bedchamber. His wife appeared from behind some drapes, from the chamber and beckoned her to hurry. The servant girl turned and looked at him with those brown eyes, which seemed to sparkle in the sunlight. He knew those eyes, for they were the eyes of Jennifer.

It was a warm moist evening on a hillside outside an ancient walled city. The plants had a Mediterranean look about them. Guards wearing armour and carrying pointed spears stood outside the gates of the city. A cart rolled past full of baskets of grapes from the vineyards. Two dirty, scruffy-looking men wearing what looked like sacks were encouraging an emaciated donkey up the hill towards the city. The full moon shone down. The air was scented with the perfume of herbs and flowers as he looked at his sandaled feet. He was wearing a toga and was holding the hand of a beautiful woman with long, dark hair. Her blue eyes were round and bright, and her smile was magical. He kissed her, but out of the corner of his eye, he saw a blinding light descend from the heavens.

There was a loud knocking sound, he woke from his dream, and opened the door. It was Vinnie. 'Pete, there's a big meeting. General Grumpy wants us there.' Caius smiled as he and Lucia joined him in the corridor, two nervous-looking MPs stood behind Vinnie.

'We're here to escort you to the briefing, Captain,' said one of them. An aide arrived, handing each of them a briefing document.

'Did you get a good kip?' asked Vinnie.

'Yes. Didn't have to listen to your snoring did I. You?'

'Yeah, good. Do we have enough intel from Ergtuk, whatever his name is?'

'Yes, we have the codes to access the mothership, and most importantly we know where our wives are now. Vinnie, we must find a way to get on that ship. We will need an X-37D,' said Caius, rubbing the sleep from his eyes. Caius could see Vinnie's mind racing as he took in the information.

'I will help you,' said Lucia, as she put her hands on their shoulders. They both smiled at her. Caius remembered his dream and the Angel of Tears, Lucia would help him find Jennifer: *she was the key.*

'What would we do without you?' smiled Caius.

Lucia giggled as he asked the two MPs, 'How's General Grumpy today?'

In the briefing room, General Scott stood up when Caius strode in and walked up to him. Behind him was an assembled force of the remaining Special Forces soldiers and vampires, each on separate sides. Some of the soldiers stood up and looked at Caius, muttering among themselves. 'It is the legend,' a vampire whispered, admiring the godlike form of Caius. Vinnie and Lucia walked behind Caius.

Scott gave Caius a dirty look, his face red, and getting redder. But Caius was different. He was taller, more solid, his eyes blazed a deeper blue, and he had the charisma of a God. 'Thank you for returning one of our last remaining X-37Ds Captain Morgan,' said the general, his face purple.

'I have returned in your hour of need. I am Caius now General, come to help humanity rid the planet of the alien plague.' The audience cheered and clapped. But the general could hold back no longer, god or no god.

'That's the second time you have taken an X-37D without permission Caius, whatever your name is. Now you have put our whole mission in jeopardy!' he shouted, as he banged his fist on the table.

'Silence!' Caius's deep voice boomed, and the whole room shook; the lights dimmed for a second. 'I have been through the pits of Hell and battled demons, so do not presume you have authority over me, General. I am Caius. I have spoken.' There were hushed whispers among the audience.

The general visibly shrank in front of the onslaught as his nose began to bleed. Scott looked at Caius, opened his mouth to say something, then changed his mind. He sat down, wiping his brow, and his bloody nose, then drank some water, cleared his throat, and stood to speak, glancing at Caius, the warrior god. He had now learned not to cross him.

'I know many of you have just come back from your mission and are tired, so I must apologize for that. First of all, congratulations are in order. In a coordinated attack with other Sirius forces around the world and our vampire friends, 50% of the alien's ships are down. That's 40 ships, gentlemen.' There were whoops, and cheers from the military personnel as Scott smiled and motioned them to calm down. He took another glass of water.

'The bad news is, our losses were 80%..' Caius looked around the room—so few—so many good men missing, brave men fighting for humanity.

'More bad news is that the remaining city alien ships have moved five miles up into the atmosphere to stop the risk of vampires invading their ships again. So, we cannot use that tactic again, unfortunately. But the good news is, the aliens cannot replace their losses. The professor has highlighted the fact that their numbers are limited, so we can take that as a positive. Their forces are focused on the major cities, but there seems to be little activity in rural areas.' Caius wondered, considering Jennifer had been taken, if the aliens were more active in rural areas than previously thought.

Caius put up his hand. General Scott looked annoyed at being interrupted in mid-flow, and his ears turned red.

'Yes, what is it, Captain Morgan?'

'The aliens can replace themselves. Some of them are clones.'

'Are you sure?'

'Yes. We captured one. Myself, Lucia and the professor interrogated him. In the short term, they can make poor copies of themselves, their clone DNA is deteriorating. Longer term I suspect they have a hybrid breeding program.'

Scott cleared his throat and continued.

'I'm more concerned with the short term, but thank you. The mothership has been tracked and has entered the Earth's atmosphere. This is now our primary target. It is currently stationary ten miles above the Southern United States, intention unknown.'

Scott's neck turned red, as he looked at Caius. There was something different about him. He seemed to have grown and aged. *Where the fuck did he disappear to—again?*

Caius stood up.

'Yes, Captain Morgan,' Scott sighed with impatience.

'General Scott, I have gleaned vital information about the layout of the mothership. There are some vulnerable points we may be able to exploit. But we need to get on board. It is too high for the vampires to fly us up. The aliens know this.' Caius paused for a while looking for a solution. 'We need an X-37D to get on board, Sir.'

'Okay,' nodded the general, his mood brightening.

'Once on board Lucia can help us navigate our way around it.'

'Good work. Sounds like a plan, Captain Morgan, sorry Caius,' smiled the general.

Professor Picard stood up. 'I found some access codes for the mothership in the information Ergtuk gave us,' he then turned to Lucia. 'We will enter these into the comms device you have, Lucia.'

General Scott is delighted, 'That's great news Professor! Captain Morgan, I want you to brief the team members before the mission, in the holo room. We can use...'

CHAPTER 11

THE PRESIDENT IS BACK

At that moment, President Wilson walks in unaided with his son Michael. Everyone is shocked and delighted. They stand up and start cheering, and clapping. The president smiles and waves at everyone.

'Young Caius—that is your name now, isn't it? Thank you for curing me with that device. The aliens are good for something!' Wilson puts his arm around his son, whose beaming smile lights up the room.

'You're welcome, sir.' Caius smiles at Michael, he reminds him of his own son somehow. His belly aches as he hopes and prays Robert is safe and well in the Welsh mountains. He looks forward to seeing him again. His thoughts go back to his boyhood and seeing his father walking down the garden path, smiling in his army uniform, carrying presents. Then his mind jolts back to the present.

Wilson stands up and gestures everyone to sit down, then he turns to Caius, 'Please Caius, sit next to me for the briefing.' Then says, 'You look different, taller. Whatever happened to you was traumatic, a transformational experience.'

Caius nods and sits down next to President Wilson who seems to be taking a liking to their champion. Caius distrusts politicians, they will say one thing and do another. Smile one minute, then stab you in the back the next—no integrity, but this Wilson guy is a genuine person; someone to look up to.

'Carry on, General,' Wilson gestures to his general.

'Yes, sir!'

The general is interrupted again, but this time, by a technician.

'Sir, excuse me, something is happening with the mothership, sir, the X-37D has picked this up.'

'Show on the main screen.'

Behind the general and Cassian, a large screen springs to life. The main viewer is fuzzy.

'Is this a live feed?' General Scott asks.

'Yes sir, hold on, trying to connect again. That's it, got it. It's over

Dallas.'

As the room settles down, they watched the main screen as the massive, ugly, gothic black shape of the mothership can be seen covering the horizon, the destructor weapon protruding from the ship, glowing and throbbing. If possible, it looks, even more darker, ominous and foreboding than the LA ship, and much larger. It looks and feels inherently evil, like it has been created in the pits of hell. A shiver goes up Caius's spine.

'The mothership looks like Bleak House on steroids,' whispers Caius.

'Yeah,' replies Vinnie, 'Gives me the creeps.'

They can hear the grinding throb of the mothership, as it creaks and groans. They can see a section of the ship that looks loose, as small bits fall off of it. Then, a larger piece becomes detached, as the vibration from the destructor weapon weakens the ship. It seems to be hanging, ready to fall. As the ship lurches, the piece falls to Earth. They tracked it as it falls, and as it gets closer to Earth, it starts to cast a shadow. Alien craft spew from the mothership chasing the falling debris, trying to lock tractor beams on it and drag it back to the ship, but the momentum is too great.

'Must be a vital section of the ship,' thinks Caius. Below, in a football stadium, refugees look up, as the black object fills the sky, several hundred feet wide, covering the stadium in a shadow. They run for their lives as it comes closer. People are running in terror as they stream through the entrance to the stadium.

Less than a minute later, the black hulk hits the stadium, demolishing it, making a crater a hundred feet deep where once stood a monument to football. The shockwave knocks the running refugees to the ground, while several nearby buildings take the full force of the blast wave and disintegrate. Professor Picard stands up.

'If the falling debris had fallen from a greater height, it would have destroyed the city.'

Back at the Sirius base, they watch open-mouthed, as events unfold on the main viewer. A technician hurries to General Scott.

'The cloaking technology on the X-37D may only be effective for five minutes or so before we're detected.'

Caius stands and points. 'Something's happening—that projector device on the mothership, it looks like some kind of weapon!'

CHAPTER 12

SCORCHED EARTH

The energy from the weapon became more intense, then it erupted and hit the Earth, the weapon moving in a slow arc, throwing up walls of fire, hundreds of feet high. On the outskirts of Dallas, Texas, a suburb of houses and a shopping precinct were incinerated, now smoking ashes where once people had their homes. As the weapon moved inwards towards the city centre, a university was demolished.

'University Park,' muttered the technician. Then, as the destructor beam moved through another suburban area, incinerating it, flames, rocks, and earth, shooting hundreds of feet into the air, the technician fell to his knees, 'Oak Lawn – my parents!'

Caius looked with sympathy at the technician, while the president got up and helped the technician to his feet.

'That was Dallas, sir! My parents are from there.'

'What's your name, son?'

'Ben sir, Ben Durham.'

'I'm sorry, Ben.'

The general patted the technician on the shoulder, and the president put his arm around his shoulders. He whispered in his ear. The technician squared his shoulders and looked at the president. Caius then understood why he was President of the United States - why he was such a great leader of men.

They all looked at the screen in front of them as it went blank.

'What happened?' The general asked Ben.

'The X-37D was detected, sir, it's been taken out!' replied Ben, who was regaining some composure.

'How many X-37Ds left?' The general sounded nervous.

'Two, sir. No, hold on!' Ben checked another screen. 'We just lost one over London. Just one, sir. It's based here, but it's undergoing repairs. Damaged shields,' he said, looking at Caius.

Scott's face went red, looking desperate.

'Just one—Jesus Christ!' said the general.

'Keep tracking that mothership!'

'Switching to radar,' he replied.

A map of the Southern United States was displayed on the viewer with the location of the mothership.

'It seems to be tracking west, sir.'

On the huge viewer, the mothership could be seen moving rapidly across Texas, New Mexico, Arizona and Southern California.

'Good god, the speed of it!' exclaimed the general.

'It's stopped, sir.'

'Where precisely, Ben?'

'Southern California. The Salton Sea, to be precise.'

'Why would it stop there? There's no population.'

President Wilson, who had been sitting with his son, now stood up and cleared his throat.

'Because the Salton Sea is the southern-most part of the San Andreas fault system, General. Quite clever really, disturb the fault line, start an earthquake.'

'Jesus—San Diego, Los Angeles, San Francisco!'

The president looked concerned.

'This base must be quite close to the fault line.'

Ben, the technician, answered the president. 'About five miles, sir.'

'Thank you, Ben. The alien bastards want to punish us for downing their ships!'

'We don't have much time, general.' The president met the gaze of Scott, then Caius, as he felt the sense of tension and shock in the room.

'Young Peter, I mean Caius, we are relying on you and your team now.'

Then they all stopped and looked at the main viewer.

CHAPTER 13

GENERAL GRIMBALD

SIRIUS COMMAND BUNKER - MOJAVE DESERT

Everyone was watching the radar track of the mothership on the main viewer. Technicians and military personnel were rushing about carrying equipment and shouting orders. There is a sense of expectancy and tension in the air as if something is about to happen.

Scott looked up as the image on the main viewer went fuzzy and was interrupted. The picture cleared, and there was General Grimbald seated on the bridge of the mothership with two frightened-looking human servant girls by his side. Grimbald was looking relaxed, dressed in his black Narzuk general's uniform, his dark eyes shining as he smoothed back his greasy black hair.

Behind Grimbald they could see an alien in braided black and gold uniform, resplendent with medals, looking coldly at General Grimbald. President Wilson and General Scott stood open-mouthed with Cassian. The president went white, and General Scott's face started turning a dark shade of red, his eyes bulging.

'Ah, General Scott, so nice to see you again! As you can see, I have chosen the stronger side.'

General Scott was apoplectic with anger.

'You miserable piece of shit, Grimbald, you traitor!'

'Now, now, Bill, that's no way to speak to your old college mate,' Grimbald feigned reasonableness, brushing his black greasy hair to the side.

If it was possible, General Scott's face turned a darker shade of red.

'You were a low life Nazi then, and you're a low life Nazi now!' The president helped his friend into a chair, as he was shaking uncontrollably. Scott's shaking hand felt for pills in his pocket.

General Grimbald opened his arms in a welcoming gesture. 'General Scott, I think you have anger issues, you should go into an anger management program, I only want to be your friend.' Then the smile left his face, replaced by a grimace. He pointed his arm at Scott as he squealed in a vindictive and excited tone.

'You will learn to serve and be obedient. I'm creating a new empire, a new world order, a new breed of half-human and half-alien. I will usher in a new era of alien domination. We will live on Earth, and you will be our slaves, *a sub-class*. We will put you in camps. You will work for us!' he raged.

Cassian addressed Grimbald with icy contempt. His eyes blazed red, and his body seemed to grow larger as he turned to the general.

'What did the filthy aliens offer you, General Grimbald?'

'Ahh, I see you have one of those vampires, General Scott, they are no match for our technology. Your Night-Crawlers will be destroyed also.'

General Scott had recovered a little and noticed the strange-looking medals on Grimbald's chest.

'What did they offer you?'

'I shall be king of New York,' Grimbald said proudly. 'The people of New York will be my subjects to do my bidding. This great city will be our administrative headquarters, to rule planet Earth. The Empire State Building will be my royal palace. I shall be a good and just ruler. I shall create a royal line that will last for a thousand years.' Grimbald sounded reasonable as he leaned forward.

'Bill, there's no need for us to be enemies, you can work for me. I will be very generous.'

'I will see you in Hell first, Grimbald!' the veins protruded on Scott's forehead as he lambasted Grimbald, his shaking hand taking a pill and drinking some water.

Marshal Zurg-Uk looked at his human colleague and smiled, he was doing well, for a human, he thought as he scratched at his diseased skin. Caius picked this up as his mind raced, plans within plans; *they were keeping Grimbald as their puppet*. The stupid fool, they were taking him for a ride. Lucia looked at him and nodded as if she knew what he was thinking *which she did*.

President Wilson faced Grimbald.

'Grimbald, your alien friends know nothing about the human race. We will not serve some Nazi-crazed aliens, they must be desperate to adopt the Nazi ideology. Remember your history Grimbald, the Nazis were defeated. We will fight you with every ounce of our souls. We will never, ever give up.'

Grimbald looked at his hands, examining his nails, looking bored.

'Ah yes, as I will be King of New York, I will need a new queen.'

Two guards usher in a sad but proud and well-groomed First Lady.

President Wilson's mouth opened in shock and bewilderment as he saw his wife being paraded on the bridge of the alien ship before his very eyes.

'Vanessa! My love! Are you okay? You bastard, Grimbald. You leave her alone! You leave my wife alone!' his voice shaking.

It was General Scott's turn to help his friend. President Wilson was upset but retained his dignity as Vanessa smiled at her husband.

'I'm okay, Frank. Don't worry about me. I love you.'

'I love you too, I will get you back, my love.'

CHAPTER 14

ALIEN HYBRID CHILDREN

Two half-human, half-alien children stand beside Grimbald. They have blue eyes, and no hair on their heads, and no eyebrows. Their skin colour is a normal human flesh colour with a hint of green. They are taller and slimmer, but there is no sign of the skin-wasting disease of their alien male parent. He strokes their smooth heads. They giggle nervously, but move away from the general, as if they do not trust him.

As Caius looks at the hybrid children the full horror of the alien agenda dawns on him: replace humankind with these hybrids, destroy the human population or use them as slaves, consume the Earth's resources until it's a broken, burnt husk of a planet. The human race will soon be extinct if he doesn't do something. Grimbald now speaks.

'These are the future now. We have hundreds more like them. We have been breeding them secretly for years, perfecting our breeding technique, now we plan to do it on an industrial scale. We have your women, over a million of them in our central factory chamber—the pick of the crop. Our breeding program is going better than expected, soon we shall have millions of the new breed, flawless with no imperfections!'

Grimbald looks back at the marshal, who is scratching at his diseased skin, then looks admiringly at the half-alien children, then waves them away.

'Now, go and play children…' There is a distant, sad look in his eye as the children walk away. Then, he turns his attention back to his captive audience, the vindictiveness returning to his voice.

'And—oh yes, I nearly forgot—we know where your insignificant little base is. Don't think you're safe in your rabbit hole in the ground!'

The screen goes blank. General Scott has recovered a little but is still shaking. President Wilson sits down, his head in his hands. He drinks a glass of water.

'Your wife, Frank! The First Lady, that bastard Grimbald!'

'Vanessa, she looks okay, doesn't she, Bill? She's a strong woman, she will find a way. I know she will.'

President Wilson stands up and composes himself. He puts a hand on General Scott's shoulder, who is shaking his head.

'Unforgivable. I lost my temper, Frank. I lost my temper, my apologies.'

'Apologies, not necessary Bill. I've always had a bad feeling about Grimbald; call it gut instinct if you like.'

'What does your gut instinct tell you now?'

'He's overconfident, lacks strategic cohesion. We can use that.' Caius cannot help overhearing the conversation and butts in.

'Sir, my gut tells me the aliens are using him as their stool pigeon, their spokesman, so to speak. He's also a self-obsessed narcissist. Reminds me of Hitler, and he made plenty of mistakes.' Lucia nods.

'You're probably right.' The president looks at Caius, then takes General Scott's arm. Scott was muttering, 'King of New York my ass.'

'They may use my wife as a bargaining chip. Is there any way we can get her off that ship, Bill?'

The general looks at Caius and back to his friend, the president.

'Maybe.'

CHAPTER 15

DOUBLE STANDARDS

Then Scott raised his hand, 'Gentlemen, can I have your attention please, we don't have much time. Our last attack was successful, but it was a low-level attack on their alien ships. The mothership is ten miles above the Earth's surface, so is too high for the vampires to fly.' He looked at Cassian.

Cassian nodded.

'So that option is ruled out. Mission parameters are for Captain Morgan and his team to use the last remaining X-37D to fly to the mothership, gain access, and then blow it up. We need to strike very soon, our window is very small. They may attack us at any time.'

The general cleared his throat from the falling dust and drank some water.

'Meanwhile, a squadron of F22s fitted with the new Gatling guns will create a diversion while you gain access to the ship. The rest of the special forces, that's you guys, will attack the alien ground and troop stations to keep them busy.' He cleared his throat again.

'Captain Morgan, you will have two briefcase nuclear devices. Your mission is to destroy or cripple the ship. Once their shields are down, we will do the rest. Let us know once you're out.'

Caius's mind reeled at the thought of two devices - he stood up and looked the general in the eye.

'What if women are aboard?'

Caius looked at Vinnie in the row in front of him as his heart started beating faster. He could feel the power rising in his belly.

Vinnie looked ready to kill.

General Scott looked sideways in a guilty fashion, as politicians sometimes do, and mumbled.

'Your priority is to blow up the ship. Er… you won't have time for rescues...there will be coll...collateral damage. This is a high-risk mission. Captain Morgan, sorry Caius. I hope your team is ready.' The general raised his chin to look authoritative, his eyes as cold as ice.

Caius stood up again, his seven-foot fearsome presence

commanding the room. Wilson looked up at him as he stood next to him, this fearsome warrior. Dark shadows flickered in the corner as his voice boomed.

'My wife is probably on that ship, so is Vinnie's. Don't try to bullshit us. Don't piss down my back and tell me it's raining!' Caius instantly regretted his emotional outburst, *he had been indiscreet, he wanted to keep his plan secret.*

'Remember the mission parameters, Captain,' replied Scott, his eyebrows raised. Caius was silent as he turned around and beckoned Vinnie to follow. They found a corner of the room, where they wouldn't be overheard. The room was quiet as all eyes looked at them; the tension was palpable. President Wilson looked at his general and shook his head in dismay, knowing his General had made another grave error of judgment.

Vinnie whispered into Caius's ear.

'Collateral damage, what the fuck? We came here to rescue our wives, Pete!' Vinnie was almost pleading.

Caius put his hand on his best friend's shoulder.

'We will get our women, one way or another. That's our first priority.'

Cassian stood up and looked Caius in the eye, his demonic presence filling the room, his eyes blazing as everyone looked at him. Battle-hardened soldiers near him backed away in fear.

'I will join you, Caius, defeater of Bael, King of Hell,' he bellowed across the room. 'It comes down to this. We either fight together and win, or both our races, humans and vampires, are destroyed. We must survive! Or die trying.'

Everyone cheered the tall vampire. Soldiers and demon vampires stood and shook each other by the hand in comradeship.

President Wilson took the stand, feeling relief that the tension had been released.

'Thank you, Cassian, my friend, good luck. Throughout history, low-tech assaults using stealth and cunning have been shown to succeed against superior technology. Vietnam taught us that.' He paused for emphasis.

'Our last mission succeeded because of that. This time it will have to be the element of surprise. A small assault against a much larger opponent. We have something they do not: we are human. Our human spirit has marked us out as mankind has succeeded against adversity, time and time again. We will be victorious against the alien invaders because we have something they do not, our human spirit—our willingness to succeed against great odds.'

President Wilson got into his stride as an orator par excellence.

'There is a tide in the affairs of men which, taken at the flood, lead on to fortune. Let's take our chances now; seize the day. Good luck, gentlemen, may God be with you.'

They all cheer at the rousing speech, even the vampires are clapping. General Scott takes Caius aside, a false smile on his face. Caius looked at him and knew he was going to try and bullshit him as he felt the lack of integrity in his voice and demeanour; he had seen it many times before. His internal bullshit detector alarm was ringing.

General Scott shifted awkwardly as he spoke.

'Captain Morgan, can you think of a way to get the First Lady off the mothership?'

Caius looked down into the general's eyes. A deep anger rose within him.

'What the fuck, General? I thought you said no rescues. What was it, "collateral damage"?'

'Well er…yes, but we do want the First Lady back.'

'So ignore all the other women that need rescuing?' Caius stepped closer to the general, a look of palpable fear on Scott's face as Caius towered above him.

'What about my wife, is she in your mission parameters?'

General Scott became more formal as he straightened his shoulders, any sign of friendliness disappearing.

'Captain, your mission parameters are to rescue the First Lady and cripple the ship. Is that clear?'

Caius took the general by the scruff of the neck and lifted him off the ground. 'By the gods, Scott, nothing or no one will stop me rescuing my wife from that ship!'

Everyone stopped and stared. Military police rushed to remove Caius from the general, but of course, their efforts were futile. With one shrug of his shoulders, they flew back ten feet to land unceremoniously into a heap on the floor. More MP's ran up, Caius snatched their revolvers, and squashed them in his hand, dropping them with a clutter onto the floor. Everyone stood open-mouthed; Vinnie, Sebastian, and Mike ran up and pointed pistols at the frightened policemen, who now backed off.

Caius then dropped General Scott onto the floor, turned his back and walked away.

'Don't walk away when I'm talking to you, Captain, I will have you court martialled!' then instantly regretted his outburst. Vinnie held a gun to Scott's head. Caius looked at Vinnie and shook his head. Vinnie grimaced and put his revolver away.

'It's your lucky day, General.'

General Scott didn't know how close he had come, thought Caius to himself as Wilson put his head in his hands.

CHAPTER 16

FUCK THE MISSION PARAMETERS

Fuck the mission parameters. The plan was getting clearer in Caius's mind about how he and Vinnie were going to get on that monstrosity of a mothership, save their women and get back alive.

That's all that mattered now.

Orders? Fuck the orders this was his family he was talking about. Caius noticed how his best friend, Vinnie had changed. 'Vinnie, you have changed your demeanour, attitude; different; better.' Vinnie nodded. We have all changed in the last few weeks, he reflected to himself.

He was no longer Peter—Bulletproof Pete.

He was Caius now. Inside he was Caius, the ancient warrior, come to save mankind, with a flaming sword, the strength of 20 men, and the charisma of a god, transformed after his battle with the demon god Bael.

And he had the entity on his side, the Archangel Michael.

God was on his side.

But he was angry—at himself for leaving his wife, at the aliens, and angry at Scott. He would use that anger to complete his mission. He would control that anger and channel it. He only had one focus now: *his path was clear.*

Cassian was taking all this in as he strolled over, took Caius's shoulders and looked him in the eye. All around everyone was still, as though time had stopped. Everything was quiet, serene. Caius looked back, unafraid of Cassian. Angels and demons, he had met them both now, the entity Michael that appeared when he called the holy sword, the demon king Bael, and now Cassian.

Cassian the demon.

He thought about Cassian. He had more integrity and wisdom in his long sharp fingernail than Scott had in his whole body. For a demon, he was a good demon.

'What is it, Cassian, my friend?' asked Caius, his blood cooling.

'Caius…I am glad you have completed the transition. You are the chosen one foretold in the book of prophecy.'

'Yes. I am Caius, he has reincarnated in me. My mission is clear.'

'Do you remember da book?' asked Cassian, his blue eyes blazing, full of ancient wisdom and knowledge, his long blond hair flowing over his shoulders.

'Yes, I remember the big, black book with the gold letters.'

'The Book of Borossus,' said Cassian.

'You know, it's funny, but until recently, in all the fights and battles I have had – I came out without so much as a scratch. Only once was I injured, during the last raid on the ship. I feel like a god when I am Caius, but afterwards I feel weak—vulnerable. King Kong one minute, a physical wreck the next.'

'You will need to conserve your energy, so it doesn't happen again. But you are protected by powers far greater than mine, young Caius.'

'Maybe we stand a chance then.'

Caius believed that he was the chosen one; that he would rescue Jennifer and be reunited with his family.

But would Jennifer recognize him? For he had changed, physically. His demeanour had changed: he was more determined, more charismatic, less cluttered.

Wiser.

Taller.

Stronger.

Caius looked again at Cassian who had a look of compassion on his face, and for the first time, Caius thought there was a smile—an ancient memory of happier times, perhaps.

'All our hopes, all our dreams, they are hanging on you now. You must find a way, for if you do not, all is lost. Vampires, humans, are done for, we will be just a memory. Remember, you are Caius. You must complete your mission.'

'By hook or by crook, I will complete my mission.'

Cassian smiled again and touched his shoulder.

'What we do in this life echoes throughout eternity, into da past and into da future, resolving karma in the place without time. Caius, time is only a linear concept in this Earthly carnation, in da spiritual world there is no concept of time. All is one, da past, present, and future. You have been given knowledge, so you will understand this.'

Caius nodded and smiled. He thought back to his dreams in a world without time, and about how his actions could affect the past and the future.

'There is one who also loves you. You have known her before, Caius, in a previous life. In ancient Rome. Remember…remember…'

Caius wondered what he was talking about, searching his memories for a connection. Then he remembered his dream. A window popped open in his mind; dreams and images of strange cities, strange people in another time.

Then, one dream leapt into his mind, clear as day. It was a warm evening on a hillside, outside an ancient walled city. The full moon shone down. The air was scented with the perfume of herbs and plants as he looked at his sandaled feet. He could smell hyssop and lavender in the air. He was wearing a toga and was holding the hand of a beautiful woman with long, dark hair, her eyes round and bright and her smile magical. He was captivated. She reminded him of…NO - it cannot be.

'LUCIA!' his heart leaped.

'Lucia? Cassian, this is a lot to take in. You knew didn't you!' Caius shook his head.

'I suspected, all is connected now, all the elements are in place.'

CHAPTER 17

CAXUS AND CAIUS

Lucia appears, silent and graceful and takes Caius's hands in hers. They are in a time bubble as she speaks. 'I remember now, your name was Caxus, you were my husband and we lived on the Aventine hill in ancient Rome.'

'You were my wife, Lucia,' says Caius, his eyes watering, the memory flooding back to him.

'We had two children,' Lucia's blue eyes shine.

'We played with them in our garden,' Caius remembers as he stares at Lucia, his blue eyes watering, then he hugs her.

'You are alive again. My husband has been reborn in you Caius. Now I am complete,' Lucia beams. Then she starts singing a love poem lament, the same one she sung as he recovered on the hillside, after their escape from the Los Angeles ship.

"Let me kiss your sweet lips again

So my soul is healed,

Let me see your face again

So that I am filled with joy and happiness once again,

Let us embrace again, so our souls are joined,

Till that day you live in my dreams."

'There is another,' says Lucia, tears falling from her eyes, recalling warm afternoons in a walled garden long ago. 'Remember Caxus, the servant girl, the beautiful servant girl with brown hair? I loved her then, and you love her now. We are both searching for her, my love.' She cries.

'Both of us need her, Caius my love, she is part of us now!'

Caius then remembers Juliana, their beautiful servant girl, surely not? The shock hits him like a sledgehammer. His wife's lover, in ancient Rome, he pictures Juliana in his mind, for his memory spans the centuries—all three of them are connected by love across the centuries.

'JENNIFER?' Then he kisses Lucia on her red lips, remembering their ménage a trois—many happy afternoons drinking wine, laughing and love-making in their bedchamber, all three of them. Jennifer, his wife now, his wife's lover back in Rome, and then Lucia, his wife back in Rome and now his lover—and fate is pulling them together now. All three of them are indelibly connected, across time and space, brought together to fulfill their destiny.

But then he remembers his walks with Lucia in the hills outside of Rome, in the warm evening air, filled with the scent of herbs. And then his murder by a filthy alien—one of the Sumeri—as he tried to rescue Lucia. His anger rises now, as he looks at Cassian, as the vampire prince breaks the spell.

'Caius, take your revenge against da aliens: fulfil your destiny!' Cassian gestures with his hand, the winds of fate now fall heavily onto Caius.

'You have many loyal and faithful companions to help you.' Cassian tries to assure him. Caius nods.

'You have me,' Lucia says gently.

'Cassian, you know, for a demon, a vampire, you are very human.'

Cassian gives one of his rare smiles.

'You seem to be searching for something...salvation perhaps?' ventures Caius.

'Maybe...' whispers Cassian.

'The centuries weigh heavy upon you,' Caius adds. He continues.

'I have met all sorts of people in my time, people who smile, then stab you in the back, and people who look rough but are true friends, a rough diamond, like Vinnie, my brother. But you, Cassian, are one of the most honest people I have ever met. I suppose you get bad angels and good demons...Cassian you are one of the latter.'

Cassian is silent as he takes it in, and smiles at Caius, thinking he is a great human, one to admire, and trust.

'It is too late for me, Peter, I am damned. But maybe one day your Patron can help me.' There is a tear in Cassian's blue eyes. Caius nods.

Caius becomes composed, setting aside his ego, looking at no one in particular. Several worlds seem to collide in his mind and focus on one point in time and space. The other people in the room are like statues, time has stopped for them. He seems to have less of the mental clutter than Peter—more focused. Then Caius looks up as Cassian speaks.

'It was ordained that you would do this. You are more than just yourself. You are the Eternal Warrior who arises every thousand years to save mankind. You are da one.'

'I will fulfil my destiny. I will save my Jennifer and blow up that ship.'

'Good, Caius…'

'I am Caius. I am the one.'

Caius feels himself believing it now. He feels Cassian, Lucia and himself are separate from the other people around him, like an observer looking on: in a different time, but occupying the same space. He feels that nature is on his side, feeling at ease with the world around him. He feels an energy rising inside him. The time bubble now breaks as he looks around him.

He is ready for the battle ahead. He will not try to predict who will win, but will let nature take its course.

CHAPTER 18

HOLO ROOM

President Wilson ignored General Scott and took Caius aside, to speak to him. 'Go to the holo room and brief your team on the mothership. We will prep our last X37-D,' said Wilson, who looked stressed and tired.

'You must find a way, Caius, the world is on a knife-edge. Falter now, just for a moment, and we are doomed.'

Caius felt a great responsibility fall on his shoulders as he thought about his wife, son and daughter, and the fate of the planet in its struggle against these unholy invaders. He looked the president in the eye and nodded, walked away, then turned around and said, 'I will find a way, Mister President.' He paused.

'My family is counting on me.'

'The world is counting on you, son.'

'If I see your wife, I will make sure she's rescued, but don't count on it.'

'Thank you,' said a grateful Wilson.

A few Navy Seals and others lined up to shake Caius's hand and wish him good luck, as he and his team walked out of the room.

They are all gathered, in the holo room.

The atmosphere was tense.

No-one talked.

Professor Picard was busy with the holographic projector. Lucia looked preoccupied with her own thoughts. She looked at Caius: her saviour?

For once, Vinnie was immaculate, his demeanour serious. He kept fidgeting and walking up and down, the adrenaline running. Vinnie knew they are nearing the end game.

Sebastian was in military fatigues but was still wearing his dog collar and a crucifix, which he ran through his fingers in contemplation. Mike joined them, cheerful as always. They watched as the professor put the alien storage device into the projector and a three-dimensional schematic image of the alien mothership was projected into the room. Caius was thoughtful.

'If we have access to the mothership computer can we upload a virus? asked Caius.

'Good question. From what Ergtuk tells me their computer is full of bugs anyway so a virus wouldn't make much difference. Besides, our clone friend says the mothership operating system has a billion lines of code; *alien code and an alien operating system.* I could focus on the vulnerable code and write a virus, but I would need Ergtuk's help and six months to do it!' mused the professor.

'Where is Ergtuk?' asked Caius.

'Scott has him locked up.' The professor shook his head looking sad.

'I made a promise to Ergtuk to help him,' said Caius, looking angry. The professor nodded, then continued.

'I have downloaded the mothership access codes from Ergtuk's data to the comms device so we should be able to access any part of the ship. I expect they have upgraded their security after our last attack, so without these codes, there is no way to get onto the mothership. Now once we're in, we need to plant the devices where they will cause the most damage. I concur with Ergtuk, our analysis indicates the weakest part of the ship is in these power plants, in the centre of the ship,' Professor Picard pointed to the plants.

'You should put the nuclear devices, one each into the two power plants - here and here. In Sector 15. Is that clear?'

Everyone nodded. Caius stepped forward to the image of the mothership, which filled the room. The blue light reflected off of his eyes.

'Professor, don't you think they would be wise to us, after our last attack?'

'Formidable, mon ami. Oui, they will be wise. For each nuclear weapon, I have attached this shielding device.' Professor Picard held up a small black box with a green button. 'Attach one to each weapon then activate using the green button.' They all nodded, and Caius stepped forward.

'Ergtuk gave me the layout of the ship. There's a central holding area here, near the middle of the ship, where Ergtuk thinks the women are being held. Sector 16. It is difficult to get to, though. But the good news is, it's near the power plants, so we split up at the last moment. Vinnie and I will go there first and get our women. Sebastian, Mike, you plant the devices. Is that clear?'

'Crystal,' replied Vinnie. Mike nodded. Sebastian crossed himself and looked heavenwards, muttering a prayer.

'Where are the devices?' asked Sebastian. Caius nodded and two technicians brought in what looked like two large briefcases.

'How do we set them?' asked Mike.

'Here are the keys.' Caius took the keys from the technician. 'Insert into the case and open. You have 10 seconds to enter a code, here. The code is 5228. Then enter the countdown here; minutes and seconds. I will let you know the countdown once I have assessed the situation on board the ship. OK?'

Caius looked hard at his comrades, who nodded. Sebastian crossed himself again. 'We need enough time to get off the ship,' muttered Sebastian.

'The difficult bit will be to remain undetected and find our way around the ship, but Lucia can direct us, like last time. They all nodded. Sebastian whispered a prayer and blessed each of the party in turn, including Lucia, who did not turn away.

Professor Picard smiled at them and clapped Caius and Vinnie on the shoulder.

'Mon Ami, Lucia will look after you. I shall stay here and pray for you. I have done all I can. The rest is up to you young adventurers. Bon voyage.'

Lucia looked at the professor, not knowing what to say.

'Bye, Uncle Louis.'

Lucia kissed the professor on the cheek. He smiled and held her hand, a tear falling from his eye, as he kissed her on the forehead.

'Come back safe, promise me, my child.' Lucia nodded. Before Caius left, the professor takes his arm. Caius is surprised by the strength of his grip for a man of his age.

'Young Caius, I must speak with you before you go.' The professor looked him directly in the eye.

'You must picture yourself escaping that ship with your wife. You must destroy it.'

'I don't understand, Professor.'

'Caius, in a quantum universe all possible futures exist at the same moment in time. Therefore you must picture yourself succeeding in your mission, and it will be so. Mind interacts with matter. You must project your mind to a place where you are going home with your wife. This is so.'

Caius began to understand.

This was the missing link he was looking for.

'Thank you, Professor, goodbye, no, not goodbye, au revoir. I will be seeing you!'

'One more thing, bring Lucia back safe, she is like a daughter to me!'

'Don't worry Professor, I will,' Caius replied. His dark mood began to lift a little, and he smiled at Vinnie, his lifelong friend and protector. He thought about his and Vinnie's friendship, he felt that he could conquer the world at that moment, with Vinnie by his side. He clapped Vinnie on the back as they walked to the launch bay. Lucia smiled as she noticed the change in his demeanour and walked beside them.

'Caius da Bulletproof and Vinnie da Terminator. Who can stop us now!'

'Lucia the kickass vampire, that's who I want to hear about, she's my hero,' said Caius. Lucia smiled and walked in between Caius and Vinnie, her arms in theirs. Caius was going into battle with his friends at his side.

At that moment Caius felt invincible.

CHAPTER 19

SALTON SEA

Hidden by the edge of the Salton Sea, two rangers point their camera at the mothership above. 'Transmitting now, General.' Back on the main viewer, they can see the mothership again, its primary weapon blasting away at the sea below.

'Sir, the mothership is using its weapon!'

The mothership computers has analysed the weaknesses in the Earth's crust and fault line, looking for a fault line that is near breaking point.

The Japan Median Tectonic line has been analysed but dismissed due to the recent 1995 Kobe earthquake, and then the San Andreas fault was analyzed. It had sufficient stress level for the next "big one", or an $M \geq 7.0$ to occur. It is further calculated that the highest stress level is near the southern segment of the fault that begins near Bombay Beach, located on the east shore of the Salton Sea, California.

High above the Salton Sea, the huge mothership is blasting it with its primary weapon. The shallow water is evaporating in huge sheets of mist and steam as the blast cuts through the water and reveals the fault on the seafloor.

On the seabed, a small crack begins to appear, followed by a deep rumble. The shallow, salty sea starts to shake, along with the surrounding land. The soil around the seashore begins to liquefy, and deep cracks appear. Hot steam fills the air then dissipates, leaving a dry seabed. A few hardy tilapia wriggle in the mud and sand of the seabed, but most of the fish are dead.

On the beach, a lone fisherman in light blue dungarees sits on an old rickety chair, his grey hair blowing in the breeze. The small crack on the seabed gets wider and deeper and then travels along the seafloor.

There is another tremor as the ground shakes. The old man staggers away from the dry sea and makes for an old wooden hut in the distance, on Bombay Beach. He stops and looks back but it is too late, as a sheet of steaming water engulfs him, burning his skin and covering him with a layer of salt.

He stands motionless, sculptured and frozen in salt, his mouth open, as if to speak. His salt-encrusted eyes watch as thousands of birds take to the air, filling the darkened sky and fleeing the sea and the surrounding area. Flocks of pelicans and herons fly awkwardly, and a rare albatross passes just a few feet from him as the shaking and rumbling continues.

On the bridge of the mothership, Grimbald grins in triumph. 'Continue blasting the San Andreas Fault. Continue north until California has been obliterated. This will destroy the last of the resistance in the western sector. Then when all our enemies are destroyed, we will bring in a new era, a new race, a pure race.' There is a mad glint in his eye as he orders another drink from a terrified slave girl. He then stands and gestures theatrically with his hands.

'I will have General Scott crawling on his knees before I'm done. On his knees!'

'I think you've had enough of those drinks, General Grimbald,' a voice sounds behind him.

The huge mothership moves northwards as it follows the fault along the southern base of the San Bernardino Mountains, now covered in shadow by the massive, grinding alien mothership.

The ground vibrates as it crosses through the Cajon Pass, the white Mormon Rocks splitting as the fault wreaks its devastation and continues northwest along the northern base of the San Gabriel

Mountains, formed by the violent upheaval of earthquakes in the distant past. The fault widens, and the crack in the earth continues northwest alongside the Elizabeth Lake Road. The road tarmac cracks along its

route and cars fall into the huge cracks in the road.

The cracks in the earth continue to Elizabeth Lake. Buildings shatter as people run screaming onto the streets, looking for safety. They scream in terror as the sky goes dark, a menacing shape above them. A water main bursts, spraying a column of water 50 feet into the air. A gas main cracks and invisible gas disperses near a petrol station. An overhead electric cable collapses onto a car, which skids uncontrollably into the gas station, destroying a fuel pump. Gasoline and diesel spray on the forecourt. Sparks fly from the naked electric cable, which is writhing like a snake as it makes contact with the road and cars. A car skids and crashes into a fuel pump; the forecourt is now awash with petrol.

The snaking electric cable hisses and buzzes as it bounces along the ground, making contact with the pool of petrol. There is a huge explosion as the forecourt bursts into flames, then combines with the leaking gas, as the street and buildings explode in a blinding flash. The shockwave knocks people off their feet, and half of the shops and houses in the high street are destroyed.

The crack in the ground widens and continues its inexorable path as it passes the towns of Gorman, Tejon Pass, and Frazier Park, then the fault begins to bend northward, forming the "Big Bend." This bend is a "lock point" where the fault locks up in Southern California. Every 15 years or so, the energy in this lock point is released with a massive earthquake.

The fault then runs through the Carrizo Plain, a long, treeless grass plain where much of the San Andreas Fault is visible, like an open wound, and now the whole plain vibrates. Pronghorn deer scatter in panic away from the vibrations and fault line. A giant kangaroo rat pokes its head from its burrow, looking around in fright.

Having moved north, the massive mothership now hovers over what's left of Los Angeles; the buildings vibrate and topple. Refugees hiding in the buildings run out terrified, eyes wide in fear, looking up at the sky, not sure which way to turn. The whole city and beyond is in darkness from the massive mothership's shadow, grinding as it circles above them. Roadways and bridges crack and collapse. In Griffith Park the soil vibrates, and the ground loses strength as large, gaping holes appear and the ground liquefies. Survivors are running terrified from their hiding places and being captured by alien scout ships as they hover over the city.

On a hill overlooking the city, three Narzuk SS Officers in black uniforms are standing and watching the destruction, directing ships to capture stray humans.

In the Sirius command bunker, they watch on the main screen as the mothership moves slowly over the city and suburbs of Los Angeles, and beyond, which are now in shadow, like an eclipse of the sun. The deep, grinding vibration from the ship shatters any windows that are still intact in the city below. Survivors, exhausted, hungry, grubby and wearing dirty, torn clothes look up in fear, covering their ears from the dreadful sound.

All of a sudden, the mothership lurches to one side, and an awful, shrieking, grinding noise emits from the ship. A section of it falls to the ground, demolishing a square mile of the city. A cloud of dust blooms around the city, survivors choking and running away. Alien craft rush to attempt repairs to their mothership - like worker bees around their Queen. Then the massive ship moves over the ocean, the vibration from the ship literally shaking the ocean beneath.

As they make their way to the X-37D launch bay, Caius feels unsteady on his feet, but then realizes it is not his nerves but that the room is actually shaking. Dust falls from the ceiling, and cracks appear on the wall. Caius feels a sense of unease in his stomach. He steadies himself as he thinks of his family and his home in Wales. What is happening there?

Will he see his family again?

Are they okay? Vinnie looks at him as if reading his mind.

'General Scott said this facility was built to withstand a nuclear blast, so we should be okay,' said Caius.

'I hope he's right,' replies Vinnie steadying himself, 'it feels like an earthquake!'

CHAPTER 20

GRIMBALD HAS MADE HIS BED

PACIFIC OCEAN OFF LOS ANGELES

It was a clear sunny day in Los Angeles. The sky was blue, a golden sun beamed down on the city. There were a few wispy clouds, a slight breeze, and at any other time, people would be on Long Beach, laughing and smiling and enjoying the sunshine, working out, showing off their muscles and surfing the waves under a brilliant sun.

But this was not an ordinary day in Los Angeles.

The Earth had been invaded by an uninvited menace. The aliens, the Sumeri Narzuks, rank and file military, and their SS counterpart looked on humans as vulnerable, as a human hunter might watch a rabbit he was stalking. The rabbit's eyes wide-eyed with fear as it ran for its life, knowing its every move may have been its last. Such was the fear in the human survivors that they hid in the crevices and hidden burrows in Los Angeles and its environs. Their sleep-deprived eyes scoured the skies for alien ships, and the streets for alien patrols, on the lookout for prisoners, to send to their camps, for *processing.'*

There was a climate of fear. The survivors had heard rumours about these camps, with many likening them to the Nazi World War Two concentration camps. People went in, but nobody came out. Stories of experiments, mutilation, and slavery echoed around the survivors of Los Angeles, instilling yet more fear and trepidation. They were especially fearful of the Narzuk SS: they are the worst, they were the ones responsible for these camps, and the kidnapping of women—the breaking up of families, coordinating the harvesting of human female DNA.

Just off the coast of Los Angeles, a few miles out from Long Beach, a massive black shape sat above the ocean blocking out the horizon. One hundred miles wide, its black, gothic ugliness blotted out the sky and the sun, covering the ocean in darkness. A few people stood on the beach open-mouthed in horror, transfixed by the creaking, groaning mothership, as it sucked up millions of gallons of seawater.

Alien craft buzzed around it like bees around a hive, repairing, fixing its structure and ferrying new prisoners on board, *mainly women.*

A stony-faced Marshal Zurg-Uk and General Grimbald were sitting opposite one another in a room. Elite Sumeri Narzuk guards lined the room, regarding Grimbald with menace in their eyes. Grimbald looked back at them. The fit-looking guards wore all-black uniforms, a Swastika emblem on their lapels, and a red armband with black swastika. The marshal's own Narzuks were too busy on the planet. These SS made him feel uneasy—Grim-Uk's men. There was silence as Zurg-Uk regarded his human comrade across the table. He had that look in his large, dark eyes that made Grimbald's stomach turn. His typically brash manner was gone, replaced with apprehension.

Grimbald glanced at the fit-looking stormtroopers in the room: Narzuk SS. The Sumeri equivalent of the Waffen SS, the elite and ruthless troops who committed many atrocities during the Second World War, of whom the emperor so admired. A shiver went down his spine; he thought he might shit himself, but he couldn't move.

The Narzuk SS had been ordered by the marshal that if he did not get satisfactory answers from Grimbald, the earth general wasn't to leave the room alive. However, these troops were fiercely loyal to their Chief Lord Grim-Uk, and they had their own agenda. Cold sweat poured down Grimbald's brow as Zurg-Uk leaned forward across the table and talked quietly, but the menace in his tone was unmistakeable.

'I have just made a report to his Imperial Majesty Herr Herg-Zuk, and it doesn't make good reading.' He leaned back and looked at Grimbald for emphasis. The silence made Grimbald nervous.

The marshal was still shaken from his dressing down from His Imperial Majesty. He needed a scapegoat now. Someone to blame—no more medals for you, Grimbald, *the Earthling traitor.* He adjusted his translation device attached to his uniform.

'I have not been impressed with your performance, General Grimbald. So unless you want to live out the rest of your life in a pain amplifier in the vaults of Doctor Vlad-Uk, I want to see better results.'

Grimbald had heard of the doctor's work, and he shivered. He was beginning to regret ever becoming a traitor now, *a traitor to his own people.* At first, he saw an opportunity to gain power, great wealth, be a ruler, with a race that had adopted his beloved Nazi ideology, but now he could see the cracks. A failing race. There just were not enough of them. Their ships were falling apart, Zurg-Uk, was a two-faced bastard, and his fellow humans had put up a much stiffer resistance than anticipated, especially this Caius fellow. And the vampires came right out of the blue. But he had to make the best of it. He had made his bed, so now he had to lie in it.

'But Marshal, we need to keep the mothership closer to Earth, closer to operations.'

Grimbald gulped as he searched for more arguments in his favour.

'We can process more human women faster if we are in close proximity.'

Marshal Zurg-Uk nodded reasonably. Grimbald loosened his shirt collar and took a glass of water.

'The humans have aligned themselves with those damned Night-Crawlers. I did not expect this. It was not in my calculations. The Night-Crawlers were just a rumour, a legend, a fable. Nobody thought they really existed…er…I did not know the US Government had negotiated with them,' Grimbald pleaded.

The marshal leaned even closer.

'General Grimbald, we told you about our ancient enemy, the Vampiri, years ago. But you did nothing. You dismissed them. Maybe I should take back that medal you're wearing.'

Grimbald loosened his shirt a bit more, but then Marshal Zurg-Uk's mood seemed to soften a bit as he dismissed the guards. Grimbald drew a breath of relief as he saw the last of them leave the room.

'Marshal, I have always looked up to you as a great leader. Forgive my lapses, I underestimated these Night-Crawlers. Resistance is harder than I thought. These vampires are perpetrating stealth raids on our ships with those spineless human Special Forces. I didn't think their small numbers would make a difference.'

Marshal Zurk-Uk leaned back again and looked Grimbald in the eye.

'Your perception of the enemy is inept, Grimbald. Our ancient enemy, the vampire Night-Crawlers, are striking back, that's the only reason the human resistance is getting results. They have damaged our London ship but it's still operational, we lost Birmingham, and the Paris ship is crippled. Rome, we haven't heard from. New York is undamaged, but our Los Angeles ship is destroyed, as well as San Francisco, San Diego, and Seattle. Chicago is intact, so are our other ships in the United States, but our losses are around 50% overall. It is a disaster, General Grimbald.'

Grimbald sipped some water and cleared his throat. 'Yes but the humans have taken heavy losses too,' he mumbled.

'Our losses are fifty percent. Fifty percent, Grimbald!' His diatribe continued.' You have exercised bad judgment in your tactics. We have lost half our fleet. But they are still no match for our technology.' His mood softened.

'Their ground forces are eliminated, and we're still hunting down what remains of their so-called Special Forces. Their air forces are 90% destroyed. We have found and destroyed their secret so-called Sirius bases. Yet, despite our superior technology, these humans have shown tremendous tenacity and great spirit. I have never known an enemy with such simple technology resist to this extent. It's astonishing. You humans, are very surprising!'

Grimbald looked nervous as the Marshal leaned forward. The Marshal loosened his uniform and became more agreeable.

'General…to be honest, I didn't expect this resistance either, as most races capitulate very quickly. These humans have spirit, tremendous spirit. I wish I could put it in a bottle, as you humans say.'

General Grimbald breathed a sigh of relief. The marshal liked to play good cop, bad cop, *but it had taken his toll on him*. Maybe it would have been better not to align himself with these aliens, even if they did agree with his Nazi ideology, this marshal did not make a good bedfellow. That is, apart from Lord Grim-Uk, his closest friend, and ally, even if he did worship a demon.

CHAPTER 21

FIND THE HUMAN CAIUS

A red-eyed Grim-Uk walked into the room and sat next to Grimbald, clapping him on the back. The marshal's manner softened. 'Lord Grim-Uk, we were just discussing our losses.' Grim-Uk eyed the marshal with disdain.

'Himm-Uk, my brother, has been trying to find the human warrior Caius. We have not been able to track this human. Reports state that he has superhuman powers. They say he has a sword; rumour has it that it is of supernatural origin. We suspect he is hiding out in one of their rabbit holes, in the Mojave Desert.' He took a pill from his pocket, and his eyes grew red.

'We must find the human Caius!' Grim-Uk screamed.

'The creature we held in Sector 1. My special project, my patron, the one that escaped, there is another rumour that he destroyed it. We must find this human, I want my revenge!' Grim-Uk banged his fist on the table, and his eyes became bloodshot. 'By the holy balls of Bael, I want my revenge!' Then his mood became more circumspect.

'On a more positive note, we have harvested more than one million human females with perfect DNA for our breeding factory in Sector 16. The breeding program is progressing as planned. We should have one hundred thousand hybrids within the next nine months. More after. The emperor's glorious plan to enslave the humans and re-populate the planet is going well.' Grim-Uk managed a smile.

'But we cannot be complacent!' he added and put his hand on Grimbald's shoulder.

Back on the bridge of the mothership, General Grimbald lounged in his black Narzuk uniform. Zurg-Uk looked with contempt down at Grimbald, jealous of his close relationship with Grim-Uk, and the emperor. The marshal then smiled as his attractive personal dermatologist attended to him. She was a half-human, half-Sumeri hybrid, and her skin was perfect. Her big blue eyes looked at her master, and her eyelashes fluttered, as she restored his broken and diseased skin using an alien device, which ran a light beam over his arm. She smiled at him and whispered something in his ear; he nodded and smiled.

Grimbald pressed a button, and a human slave woman appeared from an adjacent room standing before him, head bowed.

'Get me a drink, girl.'

'Cancel that request,' replied Marshal Zurg-Uk looking at Grimbald. The frightened human slave girl moved away.

'Why are we over the sea, Marshal Zurg-Uk?' General Grimbald asked, looking over his shoulder, annoyed at the snub. Marshal Zurg-Uk raised his eyebrows and spoke into a translation device built into his uniform.

'Refueling, Grimbald. Seawater contains hydrogen which we process for fuel. You should take a greater interest in our technology, General.' The marshal pointed at a panel, which showed energy being drawn into the ship.

'Ah, refueling. Hurry it up then,' replied Grimbald.

Marshal Zurg-Uk raised the other eyebrow. Impudent fellow, he thought to himself. 'Remember General Grimbald, you are working for us.'

Grimbald was caught off guard. 'Er, yes, of course, Marshal Zurg-Uk.' Grimbald resented Zurg-Uk, he seemed to have it in for him, *but not for much longer.*

The slave girl attended to Grimbald. 'Three more hours till refueling is complete,' spoke a subservient-looking deck officer, Erg-Ik. He looked up, not sure whether to talk to Grimbald or Marshal Zurg-Uk. He swallowed as he continued his duties.

'Ship Sectors 19, 22 and 26 still shut down for repairs. Repairs will take another 24 Earth hours.'

Marshal Zurg-Uk's face went a darker shade of green as he stood up. 'Twenty-four hours! I am surrounded by imbeciles!'

'Marshal, this mothership was falling apart soon after it arrived. It is, as we say, here on Earth, held together by bits of "string and Sellotape,"' Grimbald added.

'Where's Oluk?' shouted the Marshal. 'Get him now!'

The crew looked confused, but Erg-Ik understood the meaning, he had overheard Chief Engineer Oluk and asked him about it. The deck officers were more afraid of the marshal's reaction. If it was possible, the marshal's face turned even greener as the blood rushed to his head. Grimbald was sure he could see steam coming from his ears.

CHAPTER 22

OLUK

Zurg-Uk stood up. 'Where is Chief Engineer Oluk and that assistant of his? Bring them here to the bridge. That's an order!'

A Narzuk centurion and some guards rushed off to find Oluk.

Grimbald loosened his tie and looked at the nearby slave girl, planning the pleasures he would have with her that night. She saw him looking at her. His slimy black hair and evil grin repulsed her, a tear fell from her eye, knowing what was in store for her. But she bowed her head and said nothing. Her grandmother was Jewish, and had survived a Nazi concentration camp at the end of the Second World War. She knew what these Nazis were capable of, *this Grimbald bastard.* She brought him his cheese and biscuits from the ship's replicator. She would have a surprise for him tonight as she slipped a cheese knife into her pocket and a smile lit her inside.

A big surprise.

Oluk entered the bridge, his head held high, straightening his engineers' uniform, knowing what was in store, but a sanguine smile was on his face. He wore this expression because he knew it would annoy the marshal. He knew how to deal with politicians, with their particular brand of bullshit.

'I don't know what you've got to smile about, Engineer Oluk,' the marshal offered. He knew that, without Oluk, his beloved mothership would have fallen apart weeks ago, perhaps even before the invasion. On the journey from Ergal 5, the gravitational pull of a nearby sun caused a major scare. It was only Oluk's quick thinking that had saved the mothership from breaking apart. Zurg-Uk had thanked him personally, and given him a shiny new medal for his efforts, plus a private dinner.

What Marshal Zurg-Uk didn't know was that Oluk knew that he was indispensable, *hence the smile.* The marshal's manner became reasonable; he knew how to deal with Oluk, besides they were members of the same Sumeri social elite: the Narzuks and Patricians.

'Oluk look, if our invasion plans are to succeed I need this ship patched up in two hours, else we lose the element of surprise. The humans are not stupid, they will try to launch a counter-attack, their X-37D's are tracking us. We need to move in two hours, before we finish refuelling.'

'I need at least four hours, Marshal. Otherwise, we will need to evacuate this ship. It is structurally unsound, but you know that already.'

'Where is Ergtuk, isn't he supposed to be helping you fix some software bugs?'

'Ergtuk has disappeared, Marshal.'

'We need all the good engineers we can get,' said an unhappy marshal. 'Alright, Oluk, two-and-a-half hours. Dismissed.'

Oluk smiled as he walked out. He was counting on that. But where was Ergtuk? He was missing his right-hand man, a great programmer, and engineer. He was not like other clones, he was different.

Clever.

He had a personality and could solve complex problems, but Oluk also knew he was not happy with the status quo. He could understand that: were they doing the right thing? These humans were putting up a stiff resistance, they had great spirit. Oluk respected the humans, should they be invading their beautiful planet at all? He had his doubts.

He suspected Ergtuk was the leader of an underground political movement, fighting for rights for the Grays—the clones. He would often make excuses and leave his shift early, mumbling something about research he had to do, or an appointment. Oluk liked Ergtuk, and he was a great engineer, so he was agreeable to his shortcomings.

Oluk knew that if he reported him, Ergtuk would spend the rest of his short clone life in the extensive torture chambers of Doctor Vlad-Uk on home planet Ergal 5. No-one ever came out alive. Oluk avoided the evil, smiling bastard doctor at social events, he had the smile, of someone without a soul. Some said he had made a pact with the devil.

Oluk was a Patrician, and although he attended parties where Narzuks and Patricians mixed, he would never join the Narzuk party, they were fanatical bastards; and not to be trusted. He had some sympathy for Ergtuk and his political endeavours, so would cover up for him. He certainly wasn't going to turn him in, his personal integrity and sense of justice would not allow it.

CHAPTER 23

THE QUIET BEFORE THE STORM

SIRIUS BUNKER TAKE OFF RAMP

Caius was sitting quietly, adrenaline running, in his military fatigues in the world's last surviving X-37D, which was in an underground launch bay under the desert. There was a large, steel door in front of the X-37D which opened out onto the wilderness. Daylight streamed in showing a beautiful blue sky.

There was absolute silence.

Nobody said a word.

They all know what was ahead, and what was expected of them. He was busy occupying himself, sorting his kit, checking his body armour, ammunition, grenades and PR7 rifle. He wiped the titanium barrel with a rag, blew down the barrel and thought he could see a particle inside. He cleaned the inside of the barrel then blew again.

It was clean.

In the madness of battle, the smallest problem can mean disaster. Every soldier dreaded the "dead man's click," where the trigger of a gun is pulled, but there is no ammunition in the chamber to be fired.

Was his PR1 loaded?

Was the mechanism oiled?

Safety off?

What else? He had been for a piss already.

No distractions on a mission.

Focus.

They were all carrying small Bergen's, unlike a regular SAS mission where their Bergen's could weigh over 100 pounds. He wanted to be in and out fast. They needed to travel quickly and be light on foot, so most of their valuable kit would be on their belts: belt kit, PR7 ammunition, water bottles, medical kit, minimal survival kit, map of the ship and a few rations, that was all they would be needing. They wouldn't be staying there long.

He wasn't planning on staying for dinner, not on that ship.

The SAS would spend days preparing for battle, then attack with lightning speed and devastating firepower. *"Train hard, fight easy"* and *"Who dares wins,"* that was the SAS motto. Perfect preparation prevents piss poor performance, his SAS instructor Des had said, and he was right. Train until it was part of your subconscious and everything was automatic. He looked with pride at his SAS badge. He looked at Vinnie and nodded, knowing exactly what was going through Vinnie's mind. He thought he saw Vinnie smile. 'Only work with people you can rely on,' is what he was told, and Vinnie was the most reliable person he had ever met. Vinnie put his hand on his shoulder as he walked past.

'Just going for a piss. I'm still going to call you Pete by the way.'

Vinnie always left it to the last minute. Caius smiled. He loved Vinnie like a brother. They were blood brothers, sealed in a pact on a drunken night by the campfire on a hunting trip in the Brecons. They had cut their hands with a hunting knife and sealed their friendship. They had been through so much together over the years. Spending the summer building his house in the valley, hidden from the world, laughing and joking as they cut wood for his house, then getting drunk in the evening under the stars.

That beautiful valley; those happy times fishing with his son, chasing fish down the stream as they tried to get away, the sun streaming through the trees making the water sparkle. His son laughing as he caught a fish in his hands 'Look, Daddy, I caught a fish.' He would go back to Wales and be with his family again; with Jennifer.

He looked at Sebastian, the warrior priest, a soldier with a crucifix. His old SAS comrade had brought him comfort, solace and a sense of peace, and he was grateful for that. They had many conversations about life, God, and his own identity.

What sort of forces had brought them together?

It was no accident.

He started to believe in fate and destiny: certain things happened for a reason, the universe was not random. Cassian had told him that. Jesus, what a motley crew!

But what a great crew.

He felt confident they could kick some alien ass today.

Then he looked at Lucia. Beautiful Lucia. She wore a tight leather figure-hugging black suit, a sword strapped to her back, and knives sheathed on her thighs. She turned around and looked at him as if she knew what he was thinking, *which she did*. As he was psychic, there was no need for words between them, after all, he was Caius, the Eternal Warrior.

Her eyes were round and bright, and her smile was magical, but she was a vampire, a demon, *she would consume him*. But he found her magnetism irresistible. Lucia showed her fangs at him, then smiled a devil-like smile and turned around. She was not afraid of anything.

Formidable.

Cassian was silent, in deep contemplation. His mind was running through the various scenarios as to what might happen when they got on the ship. He was clad in leather-like armour and wore a long sword and knives. Cassian nodded at Caius, and he thought he detected a smile as if to say, "This is it".

Handsome Mike was there, who gave Caius a thumbs up, cheerful as ever, though he looked at Caius strangely, like someone he was trying to remember.

He was Caius now, after all. Not only had there been a physical change, he was larger, taller, had more muscle, his eyes were a deeper blue, but he also had more charisma and personal power.

He had the look of a god, which Lucia found irresistible, and he recalled the passion of Lucia as she ran her hands over his rock hard muscles the previous night. Lucia, his wife from Roman times, when he was Caxus, and his lover in the present. He remembered the beautiful slave girl with brown eyes in his dreams, *Lucia's lover*. His mind drifted back to the sunny villa on the hill, the walled garden with herbs, and the beautiful brown-haired slave girl as she walked past him, and smiled shyly with those brown eyes. But from the girl's eyes, he knew who she was now, *there was no mistaking it*.

It was Jennifer.

No wonder there was such a strong bond between the three of them. He no longer felt guilty about Lucia being his lover, for his wife was also Lucia's lover, and he loved them both, for they were both inseparable to him.

It was meant to be.

Lucia looked at Caius, knowing his thoughts, knowing that she, Caius and Jennifer were connected by indelible bonds of love and friendship, through time and space. In Roman times—and now, in the present—they came together through the threads of fate and love in order to fulfill their destiny. She knew she was the key to finding

Jennifer, and she would find her, both for Caius her lover, and for herself. She wanted to be united with her female lover from the distant past. She held Caius's hand and looked at him.

'I will find her Caius, we both need her.' He nodded.

There were two other vampires, Felix and Gabriel, on board, making a team of eight. They needed the element of surprise. Besides, they only had one X-37D left, and it could only fit eight personnel, but they were the best. These alien bastards didn't know what was going to hit them Caius thought, he then wondered why they seemed to be waiting an inordinate amount of time for the X-37D to take off.

He and Vinnie stood up.

'What's the holdup?' asked Vinnie.

Caius walked to the pilot's cabin.

'What's the delay Kojak?' he asked his old Yemen pilot and friend.

'Problems with the shields laddy. Also, there is an awful lot of alien activity, particularly over the last 24 hours. I'm waiting for the all clear. Give us ten minutes, Pete, sit down please,' Kojak replied sharply, going back to his instruments. It reminded Caius of the space shuttle cockpit he had seen on a Discovery Channel program once. 'Yemen was a cakewalk compared to this mission laddy,' Kojak looked at Caius.

'We made it back from Yemen, and we will make it back from this,' reassured Caius. 'Now fix those shields, all this waiting makes me nervous,' he added.

He sat down next to Vinnie.

'Maybe they're looking for something.'

'Yes, us,' replied Caius. 'Me specifically.'

'How do you know?'

'I know. I have felt their presence.' Lucia glanced sharply at him nodding in agreement.

'We stay here until they fix that shield. We are sitting ducks otherwise.'

'Our wives are on that ship, I feel it in my piss,' said Vinnie in his inimitable manner.

Caius trusted Vinnie's instincts, he was normally spot on. He put his hand on Vinnie's shoulder.

'I'm not blowing up that mothership till I've found Jennifer.'

Vinnie turned to face Caius, his old friend. He seemed the same, but different: taller, more charismatic, more powerful, more sure of himself.

Caius now spoke with utter conviction.

'Fuck the mission parameters. They can court martial me if they like, but we're not leaving that ship till we have found our wives agreed?'

'Agreed,' replied Vinnie, Caius continued.

'I don't care if Wilson wants his wife rescued either. If we find her after we have got our wives, that's fine. But I'm not going out of my way. No fucking way.'

'Agreed,' nodded Vinnie.

Caius recalled his conversation with General Scott with bitterness.

'In my temper, I told Scott about our plan to rescue our wives, it was a lapse of judgment, sorry Vinnie, I lost it.'

'Apologies not necessary mate.'

'Collateral damage, my arse,' growled Vinnie.

Kojak came over the tannoy.

'Good news, bad news. The good news is the shields are repaired but will only hold for thirty minutes or so. That should be enough to get you onto the ship. Not sure if I can get you back, though. Thirty seconds to launch.'

'Not sure if can get back. Great,' whispered Caius.

A large, steel panel slid back, showing a runway where before there was only desert. Caius could see blue sky beyond the runway. All was still and quiet as he sat there, waiting for take-off.

Suddenly, he had an uneasy feeling in his stomach. Something wasn't right. Something flashed across the launch bay, too fast for the naked eye to be discernible, but he replayed it in his mind.

CHAPTER 24

UNWELCOME VISITORS

It was black; a black alien fighter craft, but not like one he had seen before. Nobody else saw it, except Lucia.

'We've been spotted,' said Lucia, 'the alien filth.'

'I know!' said Caius as he raced to the cockpit.

'Shut the bay door,' he shouted to Kojak.

'Why, we haven't detected anything?'

'Just do it. Abort! Abort launch!' Such was the authority in the voice of Caius that Kojak obeyed without question.

'Pete, what is it?' asked Vinnie standing up.

'The alien bastards have found us!'

Kojak sounded panicked, 'I can't shut the bay door!' Then he was on the comms to control. 'Control, control, this is X37 Alpha. Close the goddamn bay door! Shut the fucking door!'

As he was talking to control, a black, very black-looking alien craft came into view and hovered over the bay door. It had the same spooky look of the mothership—Bleak House in miniature—and it seemed better built, and larger than the regular alien ships, and no doubt carried more troops.

Caius's eagle eyes could see into the cockpit of the alien craft and saw fit-looking aliens staring right back at him, but they looked different: smarter, stronger, fitter-looking. They contemplated each other for a while. He recognized them for what they were.

On board the specially adapted and shielded alien craft, Narzuk SS officer Himm-Uk barked an order. 'Display the picture of that human the one who's been causing us trouble.' The Narzuk operator brought up a picture of Caius, wielding his sword, wreaking havoc on the alien horde. Himm-Uk gazed into the cockpit of the X-37D: he could see his target. 'That's him, target your weapons on that craft and disable it!' he shouted. 'Prepare to land, I want him alive!'

'Close the bay door, they're preparing to fire!' shouted Caius at

Kojak. Very slowly the steel bay door started to close.

'We haven't got much time—hurry!'

'It won't shut any faster laddy!' replied Kojak in a frantic voice. Caius grabbed his PR7 rifle and headed for the exit door. The alien craft fired and hit the blast door, the whole launch bay shuddered at the explosion. Caius jumped out the aircraft and ran towards the smoking bay door which had now stopped moving.

One more blast and we're done for.

Caius calculated that he had about 10 seconds before they fired again. He ran underneath the steel bay door out onto the runway and clear blue sky of the desert. He got down on one knee, loaded a PR7 grenade and fired - there was a huge explosion as it hit the craft, but to no effect. Strong shields.

Himm-Uk spotted Caius the warrior god incarnate, and panicked,. But as he stood there, before the alien craft, Caius looked behind himself. The launch bay door had stuck, leaving the X-37D vulnerable; he had to do something fast.

His mind entered an altered state, the Eternal Warrior, come to defeat the alien menace, for that was his purpose. He clenched a handful of sand from the desert and rubbed it into his hands as his mind wandered, contacting the dimension beyond time. Time itself seemed to stop; the black alien ship in front of him was still, frozen in time, a bird stationary in mid-flight a few feet from him. Caius had a vision of a sword, a large silver sword, with a golden pommel and jewels, amethysts, embedded into the pommel, a dragon burning with silver flames on the blade. It had four words burned into the holy metal which seemed to be alive, the letters dancing, sparkling like lightning. Then Caius summoned:

'Caliburnus!'   'Caliburnus!'   'Caliburnus!'

Three times he said the words of power as he closed his eyes, focusing on the sword in his mind, and when he opened them, he was holding it in his hand. It felt powerful, and vibrated with enormous power, as the silver blade gave off a light. All around him was a blue light. Now that he was fully transformed into his Caius alter-ego, he felt more comfortable with the sword, more in control.

It felt natural now.

"The sword will give you power, strength and the will to succeed and conquer your enemies." He remembered his holy patron's words.

The world stood still as the sword vibrated in his hand, the power running through his body: *he felt invigorated.* And yet he was not alone, for there was another entity, standing beside him, a figure in robes, blue and purple robes, he had a smile so beautiful, and he radiated such infinite power, that Caius knelt before him, in abeyance, in silence, in absolute awe. The eyes of Prince Michael shone like blue fire, his glance enough to force mortals to kneel before him, as Caius immediately felt a rush of power to his body, he felt at peace with the world, as the energy surged through him. And when he looked up again, the entity was gone.

The atmosphere changed. Dark clouds quickly gathered, the sword shone like the sun and lightning sprang from it. Thunder rolled in the distance as Caius stared at the alien ship, back in normal time. He had one second to figure out what to do, but he didn't need to worry because the sword moved upwards in front of him, of its own volition. The aliens fired, but the blast was dispersed, by the blue protective light surrounding Caius.

Quick as a flash he ran forward towards the craft, sword blazing with silver flames, lightning erupting from its blade, his eyes like coals of blue fire. He seemed to grow larger, as in two seconds he had reached the craft.

Inside there was panic as Himm-Uk barked orders. 'Increase shield power by 100%. Override safety protocols. Now!'

But of course, it was too late as Caius raised the sword and brought it down in front of the alien craft cockpit, slicing its way through the shields like butter, then through the strange metal of the ship as sparks and flames erupted around Caius.

Then he ran for the door panel, which looked impregnable. He thrust the sword forward as it cut through the metal of the door like a welding torch, but a thousand times more powerful. Silver blue sparks and flames erupted as he brought his sword around in a circle and made a hole three feet wide.

Inside the craft, Narzuk SS troops were scampering around the craft, in a panic, preparing weapons. As Caius pointed his sword through the gap in the door, he wriggled through to stand inside the vessel, unafraid. He stood opposite fit-looking aliens in black Narzuk SS suits who gazed back at him, half in fear, half in admiration at the warrior god they had heard so much about. They had red armbands with the alien swastika symbol. Caius immediately recognized these troops as the ones herding, then separating refugee families into groups. He even recognized one or two of them who had escaped from him last time.

They would not escape him this time.

CHAPTER 25

HIMM-UK

'You alien bastards!' Caius's blood rose, the warrior in him showing its face. The crack Narzuk SS Stormtroopers stepped back one pace, taken aback at the power in the human's voice. Then Himm-Uk stepped forward from behind his companions and adjusted his translation device on his collar. He tried to look confident, but failed miserably, when facing Caius, the Warrior God, brandishing a sword that transmitted absolute power—a sword of the Gods, for what else could it be?

'Ah, you are the human who has given us much trouble. But not for much longer. I have made a special reservation for you in the torture chambers of my brother, Lord Grim-Uk, a disciple of Doctor Vlad-Uk.'

'You and whose army?' Caius laughed, his deep voice echoing.

'He is most displeased that you destroyed his pet.'

'Bael would never share power with you alien bastards!'

Himm-Uk's smile was without sincerity, the stone-cold eyes of a cold-blooded murderer.

'You have a choice, human. Join us, gain power and wealth, or you shall live out your life in a pain amplifier.'

'I will never join you bastards!' shouted Caius now in full warrior mode, his blue eyes blazing, sparks flying from his sword as he spoke.

Himm-Uk became agitated, the red veins standing out in his black eyes in his angular head, as his long incisor teeth chattered excitedly. He moved, and his troops parted to reveal a huge growling beast, a four-legged, snarling hound with glinting yellow eyes. Spines projected from its back, saliva drooling from its large fangs. It stood a full five feet high, as it advanced towards Caius, a deep growl coming from its belly. It reminded him of the Palug cat he fought in his dreams.

'Meet Karsh-Ik, King of the Hounds. He will soften your flesh…before I deliver you to my brother, a master torturer,' grinned Himm-Uk, his sharp teeth chattering in excitement.

The silver sword hummed as a blue light surrounded Caius. He stood legs apart as the hound tensed its hind muscles ready to leap, its eyes fixed on him. Himm-Uk looked on excited, as the alien hound pounced, and Caius raised his sword then brought it down with lightning speed on its head, cleaving it in two. The animal lay limp on the floor, green blood dripping from his sword. Himm-Uk looked up startled.

'I am Caius, come to rid the planet of you alien filth. Your brother will have to wait, but in time, I will deal with him as well. I know what you are, we used to have a name for people like you, we called them Nazi bastards, and we vowed never to allow it to happen again. Well, it's not going to, not on my watch. Not today!'

Caius's deep voice resonated in the craft, 'Don't move!' The Narzuk soldiers could not move, frozen on the spot, a terrified look in their eyes.

His voice had power.

Himm-Uk fired, but the laser blast bounced harmlessly off the blue light surrounding Caius. He stepped back, fear in his eyes, unsure of what to do.

At that moment Vinnie appeared beside Caius, his PR7 aimed at the small group of aliens.

'Oy Bulletproof, you left me stuck in there while you are having all the fun!'

Caius smiled, 'What shall we do with them, Vinnie?'

'Kill the lot of them. Alien Nazi filth!'

Caius addressed Himm-Uk, who had by now dropped his laser pistol, as had his comrades.

'What is your name?'

'Himm-Uk, deputy chief of the Narzuk SS.'

'Well Himm-Uk, my friend Vinnie here wants to kill the lot of you, I have seen how you treat us humans. You don't deserve to live.'

Caius looked at Himm-Uk, who looked afraid. Caius could read his thoughts. He was searching for a way out, to stay alive. He didn't care about his comrades. Caius regarded him as Himm-Uk glanced at his fellow soldiers.

'If you let me live, I can help you,' Himm-Uk addressed the mighty form of Caius, trying not to look frightened.

'On your knees and beg for mercy,' boomed Caius. Himm-Uk got on his knees. His comrades looked at him with disdain - muttering.

'I…I am sorry for killing the humans…sorry for kidnapping the women, violating them. I was following orders. I had no choice!' he looked up trying to get sympathy, but he received none.

'I was only following the orders of my brother Grim-Uk,' He pleaded.

'How many heinous crimes have been committed by bastards like you, saying they were just following orders?' Caius bellowed at Himm-Uk, who visibly shrank as he stared at the charismatic god-like form of Caius.

Himm-Uk knew he had very little time - 'Please don't kill me! I will surrender, as will my men,' he pleaded through his translation device. 'Please, please, I can help you get on board the mothership.' Himm-Uk lowered his head. There was silence as Himm-Uk and the defeated aliens awaited their fate.

'We have the codes to get on the ship already,' replied a confident Vinnie. Caius looked sharply at his friend and shook his head. Careless talk costs lives. 'Why do we need you alive?' asked Caius.

'Those codes will not work. They change the mothership access codes daily, I can help you get on board!' said Himm-Uk, his eyes darting back and forth. Caius regarded him, as Himm-Uk and his comrades awaited their fate.

'Himm-Uk, you will come with us. You will assist us.'

The alien commander nodded. Caius continued.

'Ok, Vinnie disarm the aliens, they're our prisoners now.'

'But I wanted to kill the bastards!'

'Vinnie, we are human. That's what makes us different from these aliens. We are not animals. It's important that we teach these alien bastards what makes us what we are.'

'Hmm…I understand. I still want to kill them, though.'

'You will get your chance, my friend.'

Caius looked at the aliens, deciding what to do with them.

'Tell your men to disarm and strip naked. Vinnie here will tie them up and lock them in a room.' Caius nodded towards a room, while Vinnie started shouting at the alien troops, which confused them, as they gave him quizzical looks, but then dropped all their weapons to the floor.

CHAPTER 26

A MATTER OF HONOUR

'It is dishonourable for my men to strip,' replied Himm-Uk.

'Dishonourable!' Caius was apoplectic.

'Me and Vinnie watched as hundreds and thousands of naked men, woman, and children were being herded into one of your fucking ships, bound for your concentration camps. We saw men and women being tortured and killed by your troops—in your uniform. Narzuk SS!' Caius nodded at Vinnie who shot dead two alien soldiers. The rest got undressed.

'Wouldn't win a beauty contest would they Vinnie?'

'Nah, they're ugly bastards, and they pen and ink.'

While Vinnie put the aliens in a room and tied their wrists, Caius grabbed Himm-Uk, nearly breaking his wrist.

'Wait here while I talk with Vinnie.' While Caius was talking with Vinnie, Himm-Uk rolled up his sleeve a few inches and tapped some buttons on a thin panel on his wrist. Out of the corner of his eye, Caius noticed a red flashing panel performing a countdown in the alien Sumeri language. Caius turned round and looked at Himm-Uk, saw his wrist making small beeps, then the control panel.

'Vinnie let's go. You come with us!' Caius grabbed Himm-Uk by the arm, they heard the snap as he broke his arm and the device. The alien screamed in pain as Caius yanked him after them. Smoke started seeping from the various panels as they flashed red.

'Self-destruct. Let's get out Vinnie!' As they got out of the black craft down the ramp, they ran towards the launch bay where the X-37D was waiting, dragging a screaming Himm-Uk, whose bone was sticking out of his arm. The launch bay door was still stuck open as they went inside. Caius grabbed some handles on the inside of the three-foot thick steel doors. The X-37D was vulnerable to the impending explosion, he had to do something.

With superhuman effort, his muscles tensed as he pulled down on the handles. Slowly, very slowly the launch bay door inched a few inches downwards, then a bit more. The pain was etched into his face as he made a stupendous effort to move the door, but it was still a foot off the floor. Vinnie tried helping but to no avail, Caius turned to his alien prisoner, 'Turn it off!' but Himm-Uk shook his head.

'It is not possible to turn it off,' and sat down with his head hung low, nursing his arm.

'Ok let's get inside the X-37D and take our chances,' said a resigned Caius as they ran into the waiting craft and sat down, Himm-Uk next to Vinnie. Lucia looked violent as she approached the Narzuk SS officer.

'You bring this filth onto our plane?' putting a knife to his throat.

'Lucia leave him be. He may be useful to us,' ordered Caius.

'He left his crew to die on the alien craft, can he be trusted?' asked Vinnie. Caius shrugged his shoulders.

'I'm taking a risk I know. Put your seatbelts on. That alien craft is about to blow!' Caius rushed to Kojak, the pilot.

'Kojak, close the blast shields on the windows quick!'

Caius watched as the shields on the windows snapped shut. Before he got back to his seat they heard a huge explosion, the three-foot thick launch bay door buckled in front of them but held   some of the blast force came under the bay door lifting the X-37D several feet from the concrete floor. Caius hit his head on the ceiling and fell to the floor, nursing his head. He got up and walked back to his crew, safe in their seatbelts. He sat next to Lucia, and she smiled. 'You OK?'

'Yes I'm fine,' he replied. Lucia inclined her head towards Himm-Uk.

'I do not trust him!'

'I want to use him - on our mission. He's backup. Lucia, if he makes one false move, slit his throat,' added Caius, looking at Himm-Uk and making a slit-throat gesture. Himm-Uk nodded, his black eyes darting this way and that, looking for an escape route.

But there was none.

CHAPTER 27

FINAL MISSION

Kojak's voice came over the tannoy.

'If I can get this bay door open, we launch in five minutes.'

After the exertion of the last hour, Caius rested his head on Lucia's shoulder and fell asleep. She stroked his head as he rested. No one talked; there was quiet on the plane—quiet anticipation of what lay ahead.

As Caius slept, he had a vision—of prescience of the near future, of their mission, he awoke sweating. 'There is something I must do.' He got up and went to the storage area where the nuclear devices were held.

Kojak struggled with the launch bay door controls, and eventually, it started to lift, revealing the smoking wreckage of the alien craft and blackened desert all around.

'One minute to launch,' Kojak announced. Caius came back from the storage area.

'Check your weapons again, everybody.'

'We've already done a triple-check,' complained Handsome Mike.

'Do it again,' ordered Caius. Everyone checked and re-checked their weapons, including the vampires. Lucia packed another knife into a pouch at the back of her black leather boots.

'Weapons triple check complete,' said Vinnie.

'Get your suits on, we'll be a few miles up,' Caius shouted above the aircraft noise.

'Check,' shouted Handsome Mike.

'Check,' replied Sebastian, as he crossed himself and said a prayer for the group.

'The Lord is my Shepherd, I shall not want. He maketh me to lie down in green pastures…'

The X-37D gunned forward as it emerged from the underground launch bay and rocketed into a clear blue sky. It shimmered as it flew, then became invisible, undetectable by alien craft. The runway became desert again.

'Cloaking engaged. Ten minutes to target,' the pilot shouted over the tannoy. The atmosphere was tense. They jumped in the air as they hit some bad turbulence. Vinnie looked pale as he reached for a sick bag.

The X-37D traveled at tremendous speed and was soon passing over the city of Los Angeles, then over the ocean. Caius looked down. The sea looked azure and beautiful, the sky pristine and blue. Vinnie sat near Caius, leaving Himm-Uk with a hissing vampire, Felix.

Sebastian was saying prayers, and going round blessing each member of the crew.

'Could be a one-way trip,' piped up Vinnie who also crossed himself.

'One minute to target!' Kojak shouted over the tannoy. 'A squadron of F22s is right behind us. They will not attack until you're in!'

Caius looked at Vinnie as he could see the huge alien mothership loom into view, its massive black gothic bulk filling the sky for as far as he could see. it filled the whole horizon, blocking out the sun.

It didn't look in good shape. Caius wasn't an engineer, but he could see that large parts of it were patched up. He watched as a section of it fell to Earth, heading towards the ocean. The alien craft hovered around it like bees, patching it up and repairing it, oblivious to their approach.

'I hope our shields hold!' shouted Caius to Vinnie.

'Else we're buggered!' replied Vinnie.

'Here we go!' shouted Caius, the adrenaline pumping, feeling excited, yet trepidation. Caius got into the zone, like Usain Bolt getting ready for the 100 meters final.

Caius and Vinnie looked out the window, staring at the black monstrosity, filling the sky as far as they can see.

'Bleak House on steroids,' said Caius.

'Yep, Bleak House,' answered Vinnie. 'You still remember Bleak House?'

'I am Caius, but I also have Peter's memories. Yes, I remember, how could I forget?' smiled Caius.

'Pete,' Vinnie said looking at his old friend, who had the charisma of a god, and now the strength of 20 men, but to Vinnie, he was still

Peter, even if he was a god. Caius smiled at his old friend and wondered what horrors lurked in the depths of the gothic-looking mothership. He was in good spirits, despite the mission ahead. He would need all his powers as Caius, and all of his Special Forces training.

'Strength and honour, brother,' said Vinnie as they clasped hands. 'Strength and honour,' smiled Caius.

The plane shimmered as it hovered near the gigantic mothership. Kojak had to compensate for the gravitational pull of the monstrous ship as he found a landing spot on a platform on the edge of the gargantuan ship and landed the X-37D quietly. The shields still held. For all intents and purposes they were invisible to the enemy.

Caius went over to Lucia; she looked apprehensive.

'Lucia, can we access the ship from here? Is there an access point?'

Lucia studied the laptop again, then looked out at the platform. She looked puzzled. 'Although I have memorized the access points on the ship, the ship appears a little different in reality than it does on Ergtuk's plans.'

'That's because it's a flying wreck and they're repairing it all the time,' replied the warrior God.

'Well, I think this is it, Caius.' She looked up at him with those big eyes, and he was lost for a moment, for he had seen those same big blue eyes in a life long ago, in a city called Rome, on a starlit night, humid, with the smell of hyssop and lavender in the air; when he was Caxus. She smiled again and went back to her laptop. Caius felt that everything was going to be alright.

Kojak's voice came over the tannoy again.

'We made it. I will stay here until the cloaking fails, but then I'm horsemeat. Then I'm out of here. Good luck.'

'Himm-Uk, over here, make yourself useful, help us get into the ship. 'Help Lucia!' shouted Caius. He nodded, Caius, studying his body language for intent. He was hiding something. For a brief second, he looked at Lucia exchanging thoughts, she nodded. She would keep an eye on the Narzuk traitor.

Caius made a decision. It was now or never. If they couldn't find an access point, they would have to blow their way in, and announce their arrival. Everything hinged on the element of surprise.

Everything.

Everyone looked at him. Vinnie nodded, Sebastian crossed himself, Lucia was preparing herself for the battle ahead. They could waste time looking around the perimeter of the ship, looking for another way in, but he didn't like that idea.

He made a decision.

'Let's go—it's now or never!'

They donned oxygen masks to protect against the icy cold and lack of oxygen and checked their suits. Everyone looked very tense; even Lucia looked a little scared. Vinnie looked apprehensive but battle-ready. Sebastian was holding his crucifix. Caius looked determined, confident and resolute, which is what they needed—a strong leader. They all looked at Caius for reassurance, a tower of strength giving them what they needed.

Caius nodded, and they all followed him. The fuselage door slid back on the X-37D as they stepped onto a windy ledge on the massive alien mothership. They were standing on a giant wall that stretched as far as they could see—a rock face that extended to the horizon. It was like the side of a mountain—a black mountain. Caius had a sense of vertigo, Vinnie was unsteady, then gained a foothold as they were hit by a gust of wind, it took all their strength not to be blown off their feet. Vinnie grabbed Mike before he was lost over the edge. Himm-Uk shivered in the cold and struggled to breathe as he didn't have a suit.

'This wind will blow us off if we're not careful. We're miles up here!' shouted Mike above the wind.

They made their way to the side of the black, bulky ship and held onto whatever purchase they can find. Lucia felt her way along the surface of the ship until she stopped and slid open a panel. She plugged in the alien comms device, which started humming. There was a panel of buttons with Sumeri characters displayed. She remembered the codes given to her by Ergtuk.

While the others were occupied, Himm-Uk put his hand in his pocket and pressed a button on a small comms device.

Lucia punched the codes in and the panel turned green but nothing happened. She looked at Caius, then back to the panel. Himm-Uk pointed to another button, which she pressed—the open button.

'That's it, got it.'

But nothing happened. Lucia whirled around confused to look at Caius.

'Caius da panel will not open. Think of something!'

'But Ergtuk gave us the codes, they must have changed them!' Caius shouted above the wind. Himm-Uk smiled quietly to himself, his subterfuge was working.

'Himm-Uk open the panel, or you're dead!' shouted Caius. Himm-Uk struggled to breathe as he punched some characters into the panel. But still, it would not open.

'Call da sword!' shouted Lucia!'

Caius nodded and went into a trance, another dimension.

'Caliburnus…Caliburnus… Caliburnus!' He called. But he could not focus, he was not in the zone, the Gods did not hear him. They were silent.

Nothing.

He looked around and grabs Vinnie as he was nearly blown off the windy ledge.

'We will die up here!' shouts Vinnie. They all looked pleadingly at Caius, their only hope. Once more he had to save the day. he focused again and this time remembered the priest's words that day in the woods…*"The ability to grow as tall as the tallest tree in the forest if he pleased and the ability to radiate supernatural heat from his hands."*

CHAPTER 28

MOTHERSHIP

Caius focuses once more and places his hands on the immovable panel, although he has the strength of 20 men now, this is not enough to force it. He closes his eyes and moves his mind to his hands as he feels them start to heat up. Red and orange flames erupt from his hands. The panel starts to vibrate, then the panel around his hands starts to turn red, then white, as it starts to move slightly. Caius forces the panel open. A screeching, grinding noise reveals an opening to the ship as the panel door slides fully open, and clatters with a loud bang onto the floor of the ship.

They squeeze their way in and make their way into the ship and take off their oxygen masks. a plume of stale air, and dingy lighting meet them as they look around.

'Lucia, can you direct us to where the women are being held?' whispers Caius.

'Hold on. Let me use the device again. This ship is much bigger than da other one.'

Caius looks at Himm-Uk, 'Make yourself useful!' Himm-Uk points to a computer access point.

Lucia accesses the ship's schematics, 'Sector 16, Sector 16,' she mutters as she scrolls through the mothership layout. Himm-Uk points to a section of the ship: Sector 16 on Level 4. Lucia nods grudgingly. The group huddles around Caius awaiting orders, except Cassian, who stands alone, deep in thought.

'Mike, Sebastian. Vinnie and I are going to find our women in Sector 16.'

Mike and Sebastian nod.

'You take one briefcase nuclear device each and plant them where Lucia told you, in Sector 15. But don't set countdown until I give you the signal. Stay with us until we get near the centre of the ship. We stay together until we get to Sector 16. Then we split up.'

'Ok,' Sebastian nods. Lucia gives them a map she has drawn up of the power plants in Sector 15, which they study for the second time.

Vinnie looks hard at Caius.

'How the fuck do we get off the ship, Bulletproof—without getting blown up, I mean?'

'We meet back here after the devices are set, and we have our women. We can't rely on a lift back, but I have a backup plan.' His team nods at Caius; they will follow him everywhere.

'Follow me. And try not to be seen!' Lucia urges.

'And be quiet,' adds Caius.

'Let's go,' orders Caius. Then he looks at Himm-Uk, 'Vinnie, if he gives us any trouble, *kill him.*'

'Count on it,' replies Vinnie.

They warily trot through the corridors of the ship, gray corridors, blinking lights, missing panels, the dreadful humming and grinding noise of the ship. The corridors dirty and unmaintained, the air stale.

'This place is a dump!' says Vinnie.

But no aliens yet. A million thoughts run through Caius's mind. The longer they can remain undetected, the greater the chances of their mission being successful, and them getting out in one piece.

Himm-Uk walks sheepishly behind them, black thoughts running through his mind. Lucia looks daggers at him and he lowers his head. Then they creep past what looks like a medical bay. They see strange-looking medical devices and unhealthy-looking aliens lying on beds, receiving medical treatment.

'Stay on your toes,' warns Caius. They see a large, white alien robot coming round the corner. They dive into a storage unit as the robot trundles past. Mike sneezes at the dust, and they hold their collective breath.

They tentatively look around as they re-assemble themselves.

'About 500 yards this way, then down one level,' orders Lucia looking at Himm-Uk, who nods.

'It's a miracle we haven't been spotted yet,' wonders Caius.

'We have limited numbers. Soldiers are wanted on the surface, not guarding the ship,' replies Himm-Uk through his translator, his eyes darting back and forth, looking for a way out.

'Down here, quick!' motions Lucia.

It is dark and dingy, and eerily quiet, so their footsteps seem loud. Caius feels his heart pounding in his chest, the adrenaline pumping.

The atmosphere is tense as they go down a service tunnel then exit onto another corridor. Caius looks up. The ceiling is falling apart. Vinnie treads on a piece of the fallen roof. They stop then move on. As they progress, the corridor conditions get progressively worse.

'This place is falling apart,' whispers Caius as they make their way into an elevator, just squeezing in as Lucia presses some buttons. Caius has the sensation of moving, but with no idea how fast they are traveling. After one minute, the door slides open, and they get out.

Lucia whispers, 'I think we just travelled 20 miles. It's on this level, where the women are being held, Sector 16, the central breeding chamber complex. It will be closely guarded. Be prepared.'

Caius then addresses Mike and Sebastian.

'Take the devices and put them in the power plants in Sector 15, that way. Good luck.'

CHAPTER 29

BATTLE MODE

Mike and Sebastian looked at their maps again then ran off down the corridor, carrying the devices on their backs. Caius hoped he had done the right thing with the mini nuclear bombs. He had not told them the whole story—the whole plan—not even Vinnie.

In a momentary lack of concentration, Mike stumbled, and Sebastian picked him up. Sebastian's heart quickened as he heard a familiar sound: a robot appeared in the corridor in front of them, and spotted them, then started firing laser blasts. A section of the passage was now in flames, shrapnel flying everywhere. Caius and Vinnie provided covering fire with their PR7 rifles; it took three grenades to disable the robot, destroying it and half the corridor. Smoke and flames were everywhere; an alarm sounded. Mike and Sebastian raced off again, devices strapped to their backs.

'We've announced our arrival!' smiled Caius resigned to the fact that the element of surprise had gone.

'The shit has hit the proverbial,' replied Vinnie, smiling widely. They were in battle mode now: that joy of battle felt by every warrior from ancient Rome to the present time. They were warriors fighting a battle for a cause they believed in.

In that moment, life was defined.

Their eyes lit up as they fired automatic rounds in short bursts of three, demolishing a corridor, three aliens, and a robot's arm. Their PRX rifles were making short work of the robots, the corridor filling up with the smoke and flames from the robots. Several small fires had started.

They ran forward and arrived at a large complex guarded by two robots, who spring into life. More aliens ran towards the mayhem: fit-looking aliens in black uniforms. Himm-Uk recognized them as Narzuk SS, his own loyal soldiers, *he was safe now*. He glanced at his captors, waited until their attention was diverted, then ran towards his fellow soldiers. They saw him, and gave covering fire as he scrambled towards them.

'The rat has gone back to his hole!' cried Caius. There began a fierce firefight between themselves and the party of crack Stormtroopers, who were hiding behind a large pillar.

'We're sitting ducks!' cried Vinnie. Caius looked around him. Narzuk SS with the traitor Himm-Uk were hiding behind the pillar, on their left, and the two robots by the complex entrance, on their right. They had very little cover.

'Vinnie, take out that pillar!' cried Caius. 'I will handle the robots.'

Vinnie loaded his PR7 rifle with a grenade, took aim and fired. The pillar disintegrated in a pile of rubble, smoke and fire. And the ceiling collapsed. Himm-Uk grabbed a device from one of his dead comrades and tapped a message. The Narzuk SS scattered, Himm-Uk limped away and looked towards Vinnie and Caius, but then flew back ten feet, and landed on the floor, a big hole in his chest, as a PR7 bullet hit him. Vinnie smiled.

'Good riddance.'

But it was too late, as a second alarm started to sound. Caius looked around him.

Vinnie joined Caius as he took another shot with a grenade at the robots, but the grenade exploded leaving the robot unscathed. Vinnie fired a grenade round at the same robot, but after the smoke had cleared, the robot was still standing. Worse, they could see two more robots trundling along the corridor.

'These robots must have special shielding!' shouted Caius. Vinnie nodded, muttering blasphemies at the defiant robots.

'They must have a weak spot,' said Lucia, as the robots prepared to fire with their laser cannons, sparks flying from the weapons, glowing yellow, then orange. Caius's mind raced.

Weak spot. Weak spot. What is their weak spot?

Then he remembered Vinnie blowing up the robot's head after they came out the man-hole cover.

'We have about ten seconds,' urged Lucia looking at Caius, 'before they recharge their weapons.' He could see their laser weapons now glowing orange.

'The neck, aim for the neck. That's the weakest point!' shouted Caius.

'Vinnie, I will take this one. You take that one.' Vinnie nodded.

They both took careful aim using the sight on their PR7s, and fired.

Both scored a direct hit. The two robots staggered, a look of surprise on their robotic faces.

Then the robots fired.

The laser blast hit the corridor wall near where they were standing and blew them off their feet. Caius's instincts kicked in.

'Follow me,' he said as he got up and ran towards the robots. They had ten seconds before the robots fired again.

Nine seconds.

Vinnie, Lucia, and Cassian ran behind him as he advanced towards the robots.

Seven seconds.

Caius jumped onto the robot, stood on its arm, and grabbed its head. Lucia flew through the air and joined him, and grabbed the other side of the head. Cassian and Vinnie were now on the other robot.

Using his incredible strength Caius started to twist the head, with Lucia assisting him. Between them they had the strength of thirty men, slowly but surely, the head started to twist. The robot tried to raise its arm to stop them but failed.

'One more twist Lucia, just one more,' grunted Caius. They made one more effort, and the robot's head broke, sparks flying from its neck, its red eyes dulling until they blinked out. Cassian cried loudly as he used all his strength to break the other robot's head. They collapsed on the floor, exhausted.

But Caius could see more robots coming, and more of the fanatical Narzuk SS Special Forces, whose evil black, red-tinged eyes were intent on killing, avenging their comrades.

Avenging Himm-Uk. Drugged up and looking for revenge.

The screeching alarm became louder. Caius knew they didn't have much time.

Did he have time to rescue Jennifer? Plant the bombs?

Smoke billowed around the corridor and sparks flew from broken control panels.

Cassian's moment had come. 'Felix and Gabriel—with me!' He looked at Caius. 'Go. Go now. I will handle da alien filth!' he cried.

As he stood, he started to change, seemingly taller, for he was transforming into an ancient demon, his eyes blazing red, his hands now giant claws, leathery wings at his back, his teeth huge fangs, drooling saliva, inviting his victims to meet him.

CHAPTER 30

CATHEDRAL OF FEAR

'I am Nergal, ancient demon, God of da Dead! Come to me!' Cassian spoke in deep guttural tones; the alien soldiers slowed their advance, eyes wide with fear. Felix and Gabriel drew their swords and joined Cassian advancing towards the enemy.

'Night-Crawler!' they cried, remembering their ancient enemy.

Caius, Vinnie, and Lucia ran past the two smoking robots and the noise and confusion into the huge central chamber complex.

Sector 16.

It was strangely quiet. The ceiling was hundreds of feet above them, like a huge cavernous cathedral. Then they could hear the whispers, the whispers of women's voices, hundreds of thousands, a million of them. For as far as they could see, rows of semi-transparent sleeping pods containing human women stretched into the distance. They looked into a pod and saw a woman, with her eyes open, her mouth open, trying to scream, but she only uttered a terrified whisper.

'They will not follow us in here,' said Lucia.

'The cargo is too precious,' replied Caius as he looked behind them, the Narzuks and robots stopped at the entrance, looking at them.

Air moved over them, blowing their hair. They stared upwards, trying to see the ceiling. Their voices echoed in the massive chamber, as they watched clones attending the sleep pods with their valuable human female cargo. The clones ignored them as they wandered through the complex. Lucia touched Caius's arm.

'Ergtuk was telling the truth. Show me the photos again of Jennifer and Gill.' Caius and Vinnie showed their photos as her mind searched for the targets.

'They are here! I can feel it! This way!' Caius recalled his dream and the Angel of Tears, and her promise: Lucia would find a way.

They went further into the cavernous cathedral-like complex; oval in shape and on many levels, like an Italian opera house, but much larger. As far as they could see were rows of pods and sedated women, all motionless. As they walked further, the heat and humidity hit them.

They started sweating. The atmosphere seemed dense, like a jungle.

Humid.

Caius wiped his brow, and took a swig from his water bottle, as they made their way into the chamber of horrors. His heartbeat quickened with anticipation. In the huge cave-like structure, on the far left-hand side, they could just make out semi-transparent cubicles with aliens in them. In these, they could see human women lying, sedated, on tables, with alien forms mounting them. Caius looked away in disgust, then rubbed his arm at the prickly, jungle-like heat. Then a thought flashed through his mind, and his heart skipped a beat.

What if, what if, they had violated Jennifer? Then he dismissed the thought. 'These alien bastards have no code of honour.' A tear fell from his eye.

'Alien filth!' replied Lucia.

Vinnie shook his head, trying to control his emotions, as they made their way further into the humid cathedral-like structure.

On the right were thousands of incubators as far as the eyes could see with heavily pregnant, green-skinned women inside them, wearing transparent suits, open-eyed and silent, knowing what they had inside them: not human, not alien, but a half-breed hybrid. Even Lucia was shocked by what she saw.

'Follow me. Those poor women…'

They stared open-mouthed at the scene before them. The women were restrained with straps across their bodies and are either sleeping or screaming to be released. One woman screamed 'Help me!' but she was quickly sedated by a passive-looking alien attendant.

These aliens were clones, like Ergtuk, thought Caius, programmed for medical procedures. Grey-eyed, blank-looking. Harmless.

Caius crossed himself. He said a silent prayer to Michael, his patron, for these women and his Jennifer, God help her. The clone aliens tending the women ignored the group as they walked for what seemed like miles, listening to the screams and anguished suffering of the human prisoners. He was beginning to think that he would never find Jennifer, and that she was not on the ship after all. His heart sank, as he looked at Lucia. She pointed ahead and telepathically said 'We will find her.' He followed her lead, walking between the pods, through the stifling humidity.

Endless pods.

Caius's mind raced as he looked in desperation for Jennifer.

Was she alive?

Was she dead?

Then he spotted her.

'Here!'

She was wearing a transparent suit and was asleep, lying strapped in a pod. They hurriedly open the pod and cut off the straps, Caius shook her, as she seemed drugged—in a drug-induced sleep. Caius shook his wife again, and her brown eyes half opened as she looked at him, her face drawn and pale, not recognizing him.

'Jennifer, wake up, please!'

Slowly, Jennifer's eyes opened and she put her weak arms around Caius. She clung to him, kissing him all over his face. He held her like he never wanted to let her go. She looked at him, tears in her eyes.

'I'm sorry, I should have stayed at home. I'm sorry, Pete!'

She looked at him again, as if making a double take.

'Peter, you look different my love. Taller.'

'It's been a stressful time.' He held her again.

'It's okay, sweetheart, I'm here now. We're going home, all right?'

Caius kissed her, and they both cried. She wiped the tears from his dirty face. He didn't want to bother her with his new persona yet, to her he was still Peter. Caius dug out a spare set of military fatigues from his Bergen and Jennifer put them on, to cover her naked body.

Jennifer looked at the beautiful, magnetic Lucia, a tiny hint of jealousy in her voice, but she seemed familiar somehow, an ancient memory flooded back. A warm summer afternoon, a walled garden, white drapes leading to a bedroom, and those blue eyes. Magnetic.

'Who's that girl?' looking at the beautiful figure of Lucia.

'Jenny, this is Lucia. She's, a bit different. She helped us find you.'

'Hello, Jennifer,' Lucia's blue eyes sparkled as she remembered her lover from Roman times. The happy times they spent together, laughing and frolicking. She lit up inside.

'Thank you, Lucia.' Jennifer hugged Peter again, then she looked at Lucia again, recalling a blue-eyed, black-haired beauty. *It was Lucia!* - the woman from her dreams! Dreams of love, happiness and joy. Then she fainted in Caius's arms.

CHAPTER 31

JILL GETS MADE

Vinnie was looking everywhere around him in a state of near panic. 'Jenny, where's Gill?' Jennifer pointed a finger. Vinnie was frantic as he looked around, wide-eyed, and then he spotted her about ten rows down. He made his way down through the columns of pods containing drugged, comatose women and found Gill.

She was pale and lifeless. He opened the pod and felt her wrist, but he could not feel a pulse. 'Gill! Wake up! It's your Vinnie, I'm here, love!' By the time the others joined him, Vinnie was in tears.

'These alien bastard, look what they did to my Gill! Lucia, do you still have that alien healing device?' They all huddled around the lifeless form of Gill.

Lucia retrieved the device and pressed some buttons. It hummed as she ran it over Gill's body, back and forth, a beam of light penetrating her organs. Lucia repeated the process. Caius looked around him, he knew they didn't have much time.

'Is it working?' asked a frantic Vinnie, grabbing Lucia's arm.

'She is almost beyond our help, Mister Vinnie,' she wanted to help him, she loved Vinnie, like a brother, they had been through so much, and now this.

Lucia went into a trance, as she tried to find life signs, but there were none. She was dead, killed by the aliens. She looked at Caius and shook her head, avoiding Vinnie's earnest gaze. Caius didn't know what to say. He was lost for words, as he looked at his friend Vinnie, a tear in his eye.

'Lucia… is… is she dead?' asked a broken-hearted Vinnie.

'Yes, she is dead. I am sorry, Mister Vinnie… I know how much she meant to you, I can see it.'

'Is there no hope, Lucia?' pleaded Vinnie.

Lucia hesitated. 'There is one other option.'

She looked at Caius, and as it dawned on him, he put his head in his hands. Then he held Jennifer in his arms as she started to come round.

Lucia grabbed Vinnie's arm.

'I can make her.'

For a moment, Vinnie didn't understand, then the realization hit him like a sledgehammer.

'Lucia, you have been a good friend to us, is there no other way?'

'No. I must be quick. You need to decide now before she is completely lost.' Vinnie looked at his friend Caius, then at Lucia.

'Do it. I can't lose her!' Tears were welling in his eyes.

Lucia closed her eyes, then her body seemed to grow larger, and when she opened her eyes, they were blazing red. Her incisors had become fangs as she bent down and sank her razor-sharp teeth into Gill's neck. She sucked and sucked Gill's blood, but not too much, not enough to kill her. Then she sank her teeth into her own wrist and allowed the blood to drip into Gills mouth, opening her lips.

Her mouth drooled with blood. Her eyes rolled back as she smiled the smile of a demon, for that was what she was. Lucia's blood mixed with Gill's, the vampire virus making its way around Gill's body, changing her DNA as it went, making her superhuman.

Jennifer now recovered, stepped back in horror, then fainted again. Still, there was no sign of life from Gill. She was comatose. They all stood around her, hoping that she would awaken. There was a commotion from the direction of the entrance of the breeding chamber, about a mile away. Indistinct alien shouts and sirens. They had to flee now! Caius yelled at his friend Vinnie.

'Vinnie mate we've got to move, they're closing in!'

'One moment,' whispered Lucia. Vinnie and Lucia stood rigid, looking transfixed at Gill, hoping, waiting.

Their situation seemed hopeless. Vinnie was distraught. Then it appeared that Gill's chest had moved slightly. Vinnie caught his breath. She opened her mouth and took a deep breath, her chest heaved, slowly her eyes started to open.

'I am alive,' Gill whispered. 'I am alive, I am alive!'

She looked at Vinnie, studying him. 'I know you. You are Vinnie, my husband.' She breathed deep breaths and arched her back like an animal. Vinnie noticed her eyes were different, her hair, her teeth. More colour, more vibrant. They hugged each other tightly and Gill kissed him full on his lips, holding his head. He didn't care if she was a vampire, he had her back now.

CHAPTER 32

ALIEN BIRTH

'You have a strong grip,' remarked Vinnie. Gill looked at Lucia, realizing now what she was, a vampire. 'Thank you, Lucia,' for they were now connected telepathically. Vinnie looked at his new wife thinking that there must be something of the old Gill left in there. She returned his gaze, reading his thoughts, then kissed him.

Caius re-loaded his PR7 rifle. His communicator beeped twice. 'That's Kojak. He's left, he's been detected. We're on our own now.' A hundred thoughts flashed through his mind. He now regretted not killing Himm-Uk earlier. He suspected him of giving away the position of the X-37D, *their escape off the ship now looked bleak.*

Stupid.

He shook his head. Steal an alien ship? No pilots. But they did have parachutes. Not for everybody, though, assuming they arrived at their RV alive. Their chutes were hidden there.

Caius looked to see if the aliens had discovered their location, but they were on the other side of the huge, cave-like structure. They had a few minutes.

But only a few.

He looked at his wife, concerned.

'Have the aliens interfered with you?' he asked gently.

Jennifer sobbed and struggled to breathe, then she smiled back at her husband, wiping the sweat from her brow, and taking a swig from his water bottle.

'Not sexually, no, but they put needles in us. Injected us with god-knows-what. We're the lucky ones—the unlucky ones are over there. I suspect some women were taken before the invasion.'

They can see bloated, green-skinned human women in cubicles, sweating and moaning in various stages of pregnancy. Some of the women look dead—still lifeless forms. Empty, shell-like material that looks like shed snakeskins lying on the floor. They looked at one woman as she gave a dreadful scream that froze them on the spot.

They walked over, half fascinated, half in horror, as the sweating, green-skinned woman, writhing in agony, gave birth to an alien, half-human covered in a skin-like shell, like a transparent egg.

The egg split open, and the alien baby crawled out. It had light green skin and blue eyes, and a large head. They looked on in fascinated horror as it opened its mouth and uttered an unholy scream, sending a shiver up Caius's spine. Alien clones hurried to attend to it, ignoring the mother as she asked for water, but were wary of Gill and Lucia. Caius gave her some of his water, and she smiled but looked terminally weak, her face a shade of greyish-green.

'What is your name?' asked Caius, trying to comfort her.

'I am Mary. Are you my husband?' She asked in a trance, her eyes blurred in confusion. Jennifer held the sick woman's hand.

'Poor woman. Most of the women die. A few give birth; the gestation period is nine months, the same as a human. I'm guessing she was impregnated before the invasion. The babies are born with some sort of egg sack. The aliens take them away. They don't care about the women after that, they just want the babies.'

'How do you know it's nine months?' asked Caius.

'The clones who look after me, feed me, communicate with me. It's difficult to describe. The clones seem almost friendly—unlike the other alien bastards.'

Jennifer wiped the brow of the woman and gave her the last of the water from Pete's bottle.

'How do we get off the ship?' asked a frantic Jennifer realizing their situation. Peter became business like.

'If my plan works, the device will go off and cripple the ship. Then we get off. I hope Sebastian picked his spot correctly.'

'Oi Bulletproof, hang on a minute, you mean devices?' asked a worried Vinnie.

'No, I disabled one device. The timer works, but I removed the explosive charge and disabled the shielding. It will not detonate. It's a decoy. The hidden device with the shielding will explode, and the ship will only be crippled, *not destroyed*. This gives us a chance to get off the ship. Vinnie, contact Sebastian and Mike to set the timer now. Sixty-minute countdown. This should be just enough, to get back to our point of entry.' Vinnie got on to the encrypted radio, hoping the aliens were not listening in.

'Sebastian, set the timer to sixty-minute countdown and get the fuck out of there. Rendezvous at the landing area!' shouted Vinnie.

'Roger that, Vinnie. I've hidden the device and pressed the green button, and it has disappeared. Hold on, Mike's got a problem with his device,' replied Sebastian. 'The timer has started, and he pressed the green button, but the shield has not worked!' Caius grabbed the radio from Vinnie.

'The one device will do, it will act as a red herring. Over. Just make sure the two devices are well apart. Meet us back at the RV. Over.' Vinnie looked at Caius, praying he was right.

He punched his encrypted comms device three times, the signal that the nuclear devices were being planted, which they would receive back at the Mojave Sirius base. He hoped his plan would work.

And they would get out alive.

'Sixty minutes should be enough shouldn't it, for us to get off?' asked Jennifer. 'Sixty minutes is the maximum,' replied Caius. He didn't tell them what would happen—his prescient dream. He remained silent, not wishing to distress them.

Lucia looked at him, then understood.

She nodded as Caius looked around him, a desperate look in his eyes.

'We've outstayed our welcome. Let's get out of here!'

CHAPTER 33

THE ANGEL HAS SPOKEN

On the vast, gleaming bridge of the alien mothership, General Grimbald and Marshal Zurg-Uk, Sumeri defence chief, were looking at monitors and barking orders at nervous underlings. On a large viewing screen, they could see the city of Los Angeles in the distance lying in ruins, covered in a smog from the burning fires beneath. General Grimbald was looking at his own personalised screen, translated into English, which was flashing red. He revolved in his chair, a thin smile on his lips.

'Ah! I see we have some visitors on board the ship, in sector 16. Let us give them a welcoming committee, shall we? Bring them to the bridge. And don't venture into the central breeding chamber, we don't want to damage our valuable cargo.'

'They know that General Grimbald,' Marshal Zurg-Uk coughed as he listened to the human traitor Grimbald: too cocky, too confident, I need to bring him down a peg or two, *he loved these human expressions.*

An alien deck officer looked at his screen. A schematic of the power plant was displayed; there was a blinking red light. The officer turned around nervously looking at his superiors. He beckoned to Marshal Zurg-Uk.

'What is it Erg-Ik?' said an impatient Marshal Zurg-Uk.

'I have detected a device in the power plant, sir,' replied Erg-Ik trying to look pleased with himself.

'Send technicians to defuse it—immediately. They must think we are stupid, trying the same trick!'

'I can defuse it remotely sir,' Erg-Ik said with a self-satisfied smile.

'Ok do it. But I want the area searched top to bottom!'

As Caius led the way back to the entrance of the vast and sweaty breeding chamber, he noticed more alarms going off, and activity near the entrance. Only one way in, one way out. As they got closer, they see armed crack Narzuk SS Stormtroopers near the entrance. About 20 of them, and heavily armed with laser blasters and cannons. He could make out about ten robots behind them, and clone troops behind them. Caius's mind raced.

They were hemmed in, with only one exit.

As it stood, they would be captured, or killed.

He had a solution. Not a great one, but it would have to do.

They stood in a huddle, about 200 yards from the entrance, sweating with the heat.

'Vinnie, I want you to take the women back to our RV, and get off the ship. Lucia take point, Vinnie—the rear.'

'How? How do we get past the troops?' asked Lucia.

'I will create a diversion so you can escape.' Caius looked at Lucia then Jennifer, the three of them bound by love and friendship.

'I must become the warrior again, Jenny.' Jennifer nodded understanding in a way that only a woman can understand, intuitive and knowing. She recognised his inner conflicts, his visions, and dreams, his waking in the middle of the night, screaming and uttering the name 'Caius, Caius!'

She kissed him tenderly on his lips, thinking it would be the last time she would see him. Such a short time together, such fleeting togetherness. Then she looked at him, a look of steel in her as Caius put the crucifix around her neck and give her his holy water.

'Become Caius the warrior, my love.'

They all stood back, Lucia put her arm around Jennifer and kissed her on the lips, the ancient memories of their time together drifting back into their minds, then they turned and admired their god warrior: *husband and lover.*

Caius then kneeled. He closed his eyes and blanked his mind, his mind wandered, contacting the dimension beyond time. Time itself seemed to stop, his companions around him, frozen in time. In his mind, he had a vision of the holy sword, a shimmering silver sword, with a golden pommel and jewels. Then he spoke the invocation in his deep, powerful voice.

'Caliburnus!'

'Caliburnus!'

'Caliburnus!'

Three times he said the words, focusing on the sword, and when he opened his eyes, he was holding the sword in his hand. It felt powerful, yet not heavy like before—as if he was getting used to it.

It vibrated with enormous power, as it gave off a blue light; all around him was a blue light. His companions stood back in awe. It transmitted such celestial beauty. They just stared at it, transfixed.

The sword vibrated in his right hand, the dragon emblem shone with a silver light as though it was alive, his hard muscles rippling, his blue eyes shining, his bald head gleaming, the power running through his body. He felt like a god. And yet he was not alone, for there was another entity, standing beside him, a figure in robes, blue and purple robes, he had a smile so beautiful, and he radiated such terrible power, such infinite power, that Caius knelt before him.

Lucia went down on her knees head bowed, daring not to look at the entity, lest it obliterated her, with a single glance.

The being laid his hands upon Caius's head, blessing him. He felt the rush of power in his body, and a sense of calm surged through him. Then, for only the second time, Michael spoke, in a deep, gentle, yet powerful voice. Caius looked up at the brilliant shining entity, as the eyes of Prince Michael shone like blue fire, while the others stood open-mouthed.

"I am the Archangel Michael, Prince of the Heavenly Hosts. I have existed before time itself. I was the first angel created by the Heavenly Father, and I am the one who stands before his throne. Caius, you have been sent to help humanity in its hour of need. We will not allow the Earth to be destroyed by the invaders. The creator will not allow it. He is with you. I am with you. Use the power of the sword. You know what you must do, my son. Now, I must leave you. You are Caius."

Lucia dared to look up, even though she was filled with terror, and for a fraction of a second, she thought the Archangel Michael smiled at her; and then the entity was gone. Caius now stood tall, his companions all stood aghast at the dominant figure of the Eternal Warrior with his mighty sword, surrounded by a blue protective light, and they knew that he was on a holy mission, to rid the Earth of the evil curse of the alien invaders.

'Caius,' whispered Lucia, as she knelt before him, 'Caius', she said.

'Caius, my love, what do we do? Speak to us,' spoke Jennifer in awe of her husband, turned Eternal Warrior incarnate.

'I will rush the troops and divert them. You sneak past and get back to the landing area, our RV then get off the ship. Do not wait for me. Repeat, do not wait for me!'

CHAPTER 34

PARTING OF WAYS

Jennifer was in tears, as she rushed towards Caius and hugged him, thinking it may be the last time. As he held her in his arms, he smiled at her. 'Do not worry my love, I will see you soon, Lucia will look after you. Remember, I am Caius.'

Lucia now spoke, 'Caius, Prince Michael, he smiled at me maybe there is hope for me,' she said as she held Jennifer's hand.

'Lucia, you are part of this there is hope for you,' Caius was solemn.

Then he looked at Vinnie and Lucia; they formed a column with Jennifer and Gill in the middle. Lucia took point, Vinnie to the rear. Caius raised his mighty sword, nodded towards his companions, then shouted 'Go!'

They all followed Caius, his sword burning silver flames, a blue light around him. Lightning flashed from the sword, lighting the chamber.

As he rushed towards the entrance and the waiting troops, the enemy knelt down and fired laser blasts from their weapons which bounced off the blue force-field around Caius, protecting his companions.

As he got closer to the enemy, he could see their eyes, whereas before they were confident, now they looked pensive. They fired again. Twenty Narzuk SS Stormtroopers fired at him, the blast deflected by the force-field and destroying several nearby pods, the women burnt alive in their incubators, the stink of burning flesh filling their nostrils.

They did not need to die, thought Caius, now he would have no mercy. With his left hand he fired his PR7 rifle, set on full automatic, the hugely powerful uranium enriched rounds slammed into the surprised Narzuks, killing the eight at the front, demolishing their force fields.

In his right hand, he held the mighty sword aloft, ready to strike.

Most of the alien troops wavered, but a core of battle-hardened Narzuk SS, eyes as black as their uniforms, advanced slowly towards him, ready to die for the cause, to die for their great emperor,

'Emperor Herg-Zuk!' they shouted fanatically, firing simultaneously at Caius. Although the fire glanced off his blue force-field, it stopped him in his tracks. He walked slowly towards a small group of ten Narzuk SS, with eyes black as their souls, firing his PR7, this time in semi-automatic mode, in shots of three. Five of them dropped, but the other five fired a laser cannon. The blast hit Caius centre-on, knocking him off his feet. He lay there winded and gasping for breath, his sword left his hand, clattering to the floor.

The blue force-field around him disappeared. He was a sitting duck.

He felt naked.

Through the mist of pain, he could see the Narzuk SS advancing, knives out, ready to torture him, for their own pleasure, thin smiles on their faces. Their eyes flashed red as they took some pills.

'We shall take him to our Lord Grim-Uk, he will reward us!' they shouted, closing in for the kill, high on drugs. 'Let me cut him a little first, in revenge for Himm-Uk,' said the one in front. 'Let us toy with him, for our pleasure,' said another as he touched a black statuette around his neck.

While the SS troops crept nearer Caius, Vinnie sneaked his way to the left, creeping past them. After several minutes they stopped in the corridor as Vinnie wasn't sure which way to go. They stood together in a huddle, looking this way and that. Lucia consulted her map.

In pain, Caius reached out his hand to get his sword, the mighty Caliburnus. They must be joined, or he was doomed. Only inches away, he stretched out his hand. He called to his sword, like a lover calls to his mistress.

Of its own will, the sword moved to his hand, back to its master. Caius felt a rush of power through his body, and the blue force-field returned, but he still felt weak from the blast. He stood up, unsteady, ready to face his enemies once more.

The Narzuks stopped in their tracks, knives in their hands, uncertain. Who was this human, who could withstand a laser cannon blast and yet live? Caliburnus, sentient and sensing the situation, left his hand and started to rotate, slowly at first then faster. The battle-hardened Narzuks looked on in fear as the burning silver sword moved slowly towards them. Then it rushed towards his enemies, slicing them like ham through a meat slicer. Even Caius winced at the appalling gore and bloody remains of the Narzuks.

Then there was silence.

The sword came back to him and gently rested in his right hand. 'Is this holy sword sentient?' Caius thought as he grasped its hilt.

A mind of its own?

Caius had recovered most of his strength and looked at the remainder of the clone troops, about 70 of them, who looked disorganised and frightened of this human warrior, for in all their travels to other planets, they had never met anyone like him.

CHAPTER 35

PARLAY

They stared at each other for a while, in silent contemplation. A few remaining Narzuk SS urged them to fight on. Then a strange thing happened, much to the dismay of the black-uniformed SS, the grey clones lay down their weapons, unwilling to fight.

They wanted to live.

They all stood and stared at Caius, seeing something in this human that they did not in their ruthless leaders.

Something noble, something good.

'I will not harm you,' said Caius, but the remaining Narzuk SS were apoplectic with fury as they urged the unwilling troops to fight. Five SS troops walked briskly through the ranks of the still soldiers and confronted Caius. He recognized two of them as officers directing the transportation of prisoners, men, women, and children in his battles in Los Angeles.

Cold hearted and ruthless.

'Nothing for you, no mercy,' said Caius, his voice as cold as ice. Then Caius moved quicker than a leopard, his movements a blur, and sliced the surprised Narzuks into pieces. He stood there, his sword dripping with green blood, as one of the regular clone troops walked forward, and stared at Caius. He had a translation device fitted, and looked like an officer.

'We do not like these Narzuk SS, they have no honour. We do not like the way you humans are being treated.' He looked at Caius for a while then asked, 'What is your name?'

'I am Caius,' the mighty warrior replied.

'I am Durtuk the twenty-second,' the clone replied, his voice shaking.

'Do you want to live or die?' Caius asked Durtuk.

'We...we...want to live.'

'Okay then. I want you to help my companions. I want you to create a diversion so that they can escape.' The clone nodded and agreed. He spoke to a comms device on his wrist. 'I told them you're in Sector 14.'

'That should buy us some time,' Caius thanked Durtuk.

Time was something that wasn't on their side. He looked at his watch. The device would go off in 50 minutes, then all Hell would break loose. His adrenaline rushed as he calculated they should be heading in the opposite direction to Sector 14—in Sector 12 if his memory of the map was correct. Now he had to find his companions, and escape himself. He tried Vinnie on his Sirius encrypted radio. Nothing.

Not a sausage.

He wondered where they were.

Vinnie and Lucia were whispering in the corridor, looking at a map, trying to figure out where they were, and to stay out of sight. Jennifer was taking large swigs from Vinnie's water bottle, yet she was still thirsty. The experience had dehydrated her. 'More water,' she pleaded.

'Is it this way?' asked Vinnie.

'No, we go this way,' ordered Lucia. Vinnie wasn't going to argue with her.

Gill was getting used to being a vampire. Her body vibrated with enormous energy, her mind was alive, images rushed through her head, her husband Vinnie, then a dark place, where her soul now dwelt, and she was shocked. What was she? Yet she thirsted for something. It wasn't water, it was blood! Lucia looked at her and nodded. She understood. She found a blood bag in her belt kit, that Caius had given her, and threw it at Gill. She put the tube in her mouth and sucked for all her worth. Life flowed in her veins. Her eyes turned red, her canine teeth became fangs, she felt she could conquer the world, as Vinnie looked at her in shock and trepidation. Gill's heart pounded as she put her arms around, Vinnie, her lust pressed up against him.

Lucia also took the opportunity to satiate her bloodthirst and sucked a blood bag dry, her eyes rolling white, then red.

'We've got to get going!' shouted Vinnie as he looked at his watch. At that moment Vinnie's attention was distracted, and out of nowhere, hard-faced Narzuk SS troops appeared and ambushed them.

Multiple laser blasts hit Lucia and Gill before they could react. They looked shocked as they fell to the ground. They were handcuffed and bound so that they could not move. A split second later Vinnie was knocked unconscious by the butt of a laser rifle. Lucia, though incredibly strong, screamed in frustration as she threw curses at her alien captors. They were bound and gagged. 'Your mothers are whores, you filth. You alien filth!'

CHAPTER 36

CAPTURED BY THE EVIL ONE

'Your attendance is required on the bridge,' spoke a haughty black-uniformed Narzuk SS officer, his black eyes glinting as he thought of the best method of torture for his new prizes. Red veins bulged in his jet-black eyes, as he toyed with a macabre black figurine around his neck.

'Where is the human Caius – for I have unfinished business with him?'

The haughty Narzuk officer, turned his attention to Gill, and started to stroke her hair, and feel her body and breasts - she bared her fangs at him and struggled to escape. As Vinnie gazed at him through a mist of pain, he thought he recognized him.

Had he seen him in New York with the traitor Grimbald?

Yes, he had!

And again in LA, supervising the loading of captives onto ships. His captor's pale green skin seemed healthier than the rank and file Narzuks, and he took an instant dislike to him, *fuckface,* that was his nickname now. The slimy shit was in the same class as *shitface,* the lieutenant who tried to dismiss him from the service, as the hate grew in his heart.

He looked at his watch: 40 minutes to zero hour. He had been through interrogation, he knew the drill, but they needed to escape and get off the ship, and if he could kill *fuckface* first, that would be a bonus.

He would bide his time. His head spun, and then he fell unconscious.

When he awoke, he was lying on the floor on the bridge of the mothership: huge, gleaming white and full of alien computer screens. There were many red centurion bridge guards, a few Narzuks and many clone troops. His head was spinning and he had a severe headache. He could see his companions on the floor next to him; Gill moved next to him and tried to kiss him. He moved closer and kissed her red vampire lips, but then he felt the butt of a laser rifle in his ribs, as he saw *fuckface* grinning at him.

But where was his blood brother, Caius, and Cassian for that matter? He couldn't see them. It all seemed hopeless. Soon the ship would blow with them on it.

That wasn't the plan.

Where was Caius?

Marshal Zurg-Uk casually stood up and walked towards them.

'Get them to their feet,' he ordered. As they were stood up, Vinnie could see they were surrounded by crack Narzuk SS troops. He saw the marshal in front of him, and in the background, he recognised General Grimbald, the traitor, the Judas who had betrayed his people, his race.

Marshal Zurg-Uk looked with disdain at Vinnie and adjusted his translator.

'I am Marshal Zurg-Uk. Where is the human, the one called Caius?'

'Oh you will not catch him,' replied Vinnie.

'Where is the human troublemaker, for I wish to speak with him?' the haughty Narzuk SS officer replied, retaining his confidence, 'and remove those cursed crosses around their necks, *they offend me!*'

Zurg-Uk knew this officer reported directly to the emperor, one of his inner circle. He knew he couldn't touch him, the emperor would be displeased.

The Marshal looked again at Vinnie.

'Let me introduce Lord Grim-Uk. He has some very special skills.'

'I am Lord Grim-Uk,' *fuckface's* smile reminded Vinnie of old black-and-white documentary films of Himmler, the evil Nazi in charge of the Holocaust, one of Hitler's lieutenants, and a member of his Inner Circle. He looked at the empty black eyes, devoid of compassion, committer of unknown heinous crimes against other races, and the red veins running through them.

A smile of pure evil.

Yes, he was the one standing next to Grimbald in New York, as he made the Nazi speech.

'Human, I am a disciple of Doctor Vlad-Uk on home planet Ergal 5. He taught me all his techniques in his torture chambers. We have excellent facilities on this ship, human, and it will be my pleasure to extract your secrets, slowly, but inevitably. I swear, as Bael is my witness!' he said, as he toyed with his obscene black pendant.

'You will not get anything out of me,' replied Vinnie, as a shiver went down his spine. On a black ops mission, if he was captured, *(and luckily it had never happened)*, his resistance to interrogation training taught him never to reveal who he was, and to be polite to his captors, however much they beat him, however much he hated them, however much they tortured him.

But for this bastard, *fuckface*, he couldn't control his feelings.

'Go fuck yourself!' shouted Vinnie, through his pain.

'What were you doing on our ship?' Grim-Uk leaned closer. Vinnie couldn't see his watch as his hands were tied behind his back, but he reckoned on 30 minutes till zero hour.

'Where is the one called Caius? He killed my brother, and I wish to take revenge. And he offended my patron Bael. SPEAK human!'

Grim-Uk's sharp teeth chattered in anger and frustration, the saliva dripping onto Vinnie's face.

Grim-Uk kicked Vinnie in the ribs again with his black boots.

'We have defused your silly little bomb, Earthling,' added Grim-Uk.

The alien bastards hadn't a clue as Vinnie smiled inside.

Caius where are you?

He was answered by a thud on the blast doors outside the bridge.

Then a louder thud. The Sumeri bridge crew looked startled.

'Seal the inner blast doors!' ordered Marshal Zurg-Uk.

CHAPTER 37

CONFRONTATION WITH THE TRAITOR

A secondary door closed behind the main door, sealing them in the bridge.

Vinnie smiled. Caius is coming. His blood brother.

'Your upstart human will not be able to break through that door,' spoke Zurg-Uk confidently. The Narzuk officers appeared less confident and looked towards the direction of the blast door, fear etched into their faces.

Vinnie smiled again.

On the other side of the door, Caius held Caliburnus aloft, as it glowed with a silvery blue light, and started to hum, quietly, then louder. The silvery blue aura became brighter and denser as the whole corridor seemed to shake. The holy sword vibrated in his hands. It took all his strength to control it. Then he decided to let it do its bidding—to let it flow. The sword came down on the door and went through it like a knife through butter. It went through three feet of the doors, the outer blast door, the main door, and then the inner blast door, which erupted in sparks and orange and red flames. Then Caius brought the sword round in an arc and made a hole he could get through.

He stepped through and surveyed the scene.

He was surrounded by Narzuk SS and red centurions, the elite, and there were his friends and wife, held captive. He stood there before them, bald-headed, over seven feet tall now, blue eyes smouldering fire, emanating the charisma of a Greek god. His sleeves had been ripped in the fighting and showed his rippling muscles. Dark shadows appeared, and thunder rumbled, and the bridge shook. Lightning erupted from the sword, torching several clones, a red uniformed centurion, and two Narzuks, who stood nearby. The smell of burning flesh started to fill the bridge, as the troops gazed in fear at the mighty figure of Caius and his powerful sword.

Everyone stared at him. The clones backed away, while the Narzuk

SS and centurions stood their ground. General Grimbald got up from his chair and walked towards Caius, trying to look confident, but glancing nervously at the shining supernatural sword.

As Caius advanced towards his friends in the central command centre of the alien invasion, he noticed a portrait of Hitler on a white wall, and a woman's portrait next to it. As he got nearer, he noticed Grimbald's starched Narzuk uniform, decorated with alien medals, and then looked at the picture of Hitler again.

It sent shivers down his spine.

It cannot be.

Grimbald's features: Hitler? Grimbald?

He wanted answers. He would kill him after.

There was a resemblance. There was definitely a resemblance. Why did no one spot it before? Now Caius knew Grimbald was an evil bastard and he had to stop him.

At any cost.

Grimbald stood next to Grim-Uk and they watched Caius unsure what to do, then Grimbald regained some confidence, as he stood to address the warrior god. 'Are you the one called Caius?' Grim-Uk's eyes flashed red.

'Yes, I am Caius, I have been called to rid the Earth of the Sumeri vermin—and traitors!' His deep voice echoed and reverberated throughout the large bridge area. The regular grey-eyed clone soldiers stepped back again in fear again.

Grimbald nodded patronisingly, then looked at Hitler's portrait.

'Caius, welcome to my bridge, on this great occasion. I am General Grimbald. I can see you like my paintings. We're related, you know…on my grandmother's side of the family. Paula—the Fuhrer's beloved sister. Adolf Hitler was my great uncle. Paula was my grandmother,' he said proudly.

Caius joined his companions as the guards moved away. He and Vinnie stood open-mouthed in disbelief, at the revelation.

While all eyes were on Caius, nobody noticed Cassian sliding through the hole in the door.

'Nazi bastard…' Vinnie muttered under his breath. Caius put a hand on his arm. He wanted to hear the traitor speak, trying to make sense of it all. A look of self-satisfaction came over Grimbald's face as he continued.

Marshal Zurg-Uk shooed away his skin doctor as he focused his attention on the upstart Grimbald. The Narzuk SS, they could no longer be trusted, so he nodded to his own loyal Narzuk troops, to close in on the human infiltrators on his bridge. Just one slip up Earthling traitor—just one. Zurg-Uk now regretted the decision made by his beloved but misguided emperor to give Grimbald so much power.

The human traitor ingratiating himself with the emperor—just because he was a blood relative of Hitler, his emperor taking it all in, *the old fool.* He should have been in full charge of this mission, Marshal Zurg-Uk, instead of sharing it with the human traitor, the imposter, General Grimbald, and his ridiculous Nazi ideology.

Grimbald now continued his oratory, getting into his stride.

'Now, what occasion, you may ask? We are destroying California by disrupting the San Andreas Fault. Yes, and we know where your miserable little base is, you can't hide from us.' A thread of hate was apparent in his voice. 'A fleet of fighter craft is attacking it as we speak.' Grimbald's voice became vindictive.

'You are completely alone. Your situation is hopeless.' The traitor showed his yellow teeth. Grimbald emphasised the last point smiling, as if he had won the war.

Grimbald paused and gave a victorious smile. Over-confident, thought Caius, they don't know what's coming. But they must get off the ship. A bead of sweat fell from his brow as his mind raced for a way they could get out alive. But first, he wanted to kill Grimbald, the one who had betrayed his people. And that evil bastard Grim-Uk, the war criminal. He glanced at Lucia; they communicate silently. She nodded. She knows something, yes, Cassian is here, waiting in the shadows.

Bide your time.

But there is no time left.

Twenty-two minutes.

Grimbald gestured ostentatiously.

'Have a chair and—where are my manners? Get them a drink, this alien alcohol is quite good you know. They have replicators. I can have any food or drink I fancy. You see, Caius, we are planning a new world order, a new breed of half-human half-alien. A supreme race to replace humans. We will create an empire and rule for 1000 years.'

Caius couldn't contain himself any longer as his voice boomed.

'You sound just like Hitler. Things didn't turn out too well for him either! You, Nazi bastard, you kidnap my wife for your so-called supreme "fucking" race! My wife! We will never be your slaves, Grimbald, not while I have an ounce of strength to resist you. We're human, we may have our faults, but we always win through. Do you know why?' Caius paused glowering at his enemies.

'Because of our human spirit!' the bridge shuddered at his voice.

Caius now looked behind Grimbald to the imposing figure of Marshal Zurg-Uk, who now spoke, adjusting his translator.

'I must admit you humans do have spirit—a worthy opponent. I remember the race of Ergal 6 we conquered. Myself and Lord Grim-Uk here massacred ten million and put the rest into slavery. Pathetic race. But you humans, I salute you. You put up a great fight before you die!' The marshal leaned forward, a hint of vindictiveness in his voice.

'But you, Caius, we need men like you, men of courage, and strength,' he smiled, sounding reasonable.

Grimbald now gestured with open arms towards Caius. Grim-Uk was impassive as he toyed with the black figurine of his god around his neck, angry about the loss of his diabolical patron.

CHAPTER 38

THE TEMPTATION OF CAIUS

'Our illustrious marshal is correct. There is no need for us to be enemies, Caius. We can be partners you and me – we welcome a human of your talents in the new order. I can offer you a position of power.'

Grimbald looked at Zurg-Uk. The marshal nodded in agreement. Grimbald went to a panel and pressed a button showing him all the countries of the world, in all their glory. How about England, Caius? I can make you King of England. All you have to do is kneel down before me and vow your loyalty to our cause. Just one act of worship, that is all I ask,' he asked, feigning reasonableness with open arms, his lank black hair falling over his face, his shifty eyes darting at Grim-Uk.

'Not in a million years, Grimbald, England already has a Queen, and my loyalty is to her, God bless her.' Grimbald looked disappointed as he now leered at Jennifer and Gill, licking his lips, the vindictiveness returning to his tone.

'You disappoint me, Caius. You have made a big mistake.' Grimbald nodded to Grim-Uk.

Grimbald gestured casually, and the First Lady was brought to the bridge from a side room.

'The First Lady! Are you okay?' asked Caius in shock.

Vanessa nodded, but she was tearful. She was well dressed and groomed, trying to retain a sense of composure. A huge grin spread across Grimbald's face.

'Let me introduce you to my new queen. It's only fitting that, as the future king of New York, I shall need a queen. Take a seat next to me, my dear Vanessa.'

Vanessa sat next to Grimbald, a look of disgust on her face, but managed to keep herself together. Grimbald looked at Caius, hoping to bait him.

'Now then, Caius, I see your women have not yet sampled the delights of our males, but I'm sure we can oblige you.'

Caius's warrior blood surged at the insult. Jennifer stepped forward and unleashed her tongue at Grimbald.

'Drop dead, you fucking Nazi!'

Even Caius was caught by the ferocity of her verbal onslaught. Grimbald, taken aback, now responded. 'Now, now, that's no way to talk, maybe I can taste you first. You can be my mistress!'

Caius couldn't contain himself any longer.

'You leave my wife alone! I've been to Hell and back to rescue my wife, she stays with me,' his voice boomed throughout the bridge. Even the fanatical Narzuk SS stepped back from him.

Cassian, hiding in the shadows, silent as stone, now stepped forward. Even the Narzuk SS moved back, a look of fear in their eyes, for they recognised their ancient enemy.

'My friend Caius here is correct. You are over-confident. It has always been a failing in mad dictators, like yourself,' spoke Cassian, remembering his escapades helping the French Resistance fight the Nazis during the Second World War.

Grimbald looked at Cassian and Lucia, a look of loathing in his eyes. 'As for you Night-Crawlers, you will serve me also. Serve or die!' he said, showing his yellow teeth.

The eyes of Cassian turned a shade of red, as if he were a demon woken from a deep slumber. Fifty laser pistols were now pointing at Lucia and Cassian. Caius motioned his hand for them to back off.

Cassian grew larger, his eyes a darker shade of red. The alien guards who are standing with him moved away nervously, but Grimbald was so caught up in the moment, he did not notice. The SS Narzuks closed in on Cassian, prompted by Grim-Uk, remembering his promise to the emperor.

Caius now regretted his emotional outburst as he stealthily glanced at his stopwatch and was counting down. Ten minutes to go to detonation.

He needed to buy time. He changed tack.

'Grimbald, maybe you are right, and our cause is lost, and we should join forces.' Some of the tension was released, and some of the SS moved back. Grimbald smiled with open arms, but Vinnie was shocked. He couldn't believe what his brother Caius was saying.

But Lucia and Cassian nodded, understanding his ploy.

CHAPTER 39

ART OF WAR

Play along with Grimbald, Caius whispered to Gill and Jennifer, *keep him talking.* He was desperate to keep the aliens occupied. *Distraction and diversion* —he had read the Art of War.

Jennifer's demeanour changed, and she smiles at Grimbald, understanding her husband's subterfuge.

'Actually, I would like a drink please, I'm so thirsty. I must say, I like your uniform. I like a man in uniform.'

Gill, who was now a vampire, composed herself, controlling her instincts to leap upon Grimbald and tear his throat out.

'I will have a drink too,' she said, pretending to be human.

Grimbald positively beamed.

'Of course ladies, of course, come and sit by me.'

Zurg-Uk's eyes rolled in displeasure, smelling a rat.

Jennifer sat on the other side of Vanessa, who looked confused, but gave a wry smile at Jennifer, knowing they were planning something. Jennifer leaned towards Grimbald.

'Your uniform looks so stiff. Let me loosen it for you.'

Gill looked at Grimbald's uniform and pursed her lips erotically.

'Ooh, is that a gun in your pocket or are you just pleased to see me?'

A big smile appeared on Grimbald's oily face. He was lapping it up.

Excellent, thought Caius…just keep the bastard distracted, *just a few more minutes.*

CHAPTER 40

DEUS EX MACHINA

'**S**ilence!' ordered Marshal Zurg-Uk testily. 'Enough of this nonsense!'

Caius glanced at his watch.

Five minutes to zero hour.

Then Caliburnus, his holy sword, suddenly disappeared. The sword definitely had a mind of its own. Caius was uncertain and felt naked, and weak. He staggered.

The Narzuk SS edged closer to their enemy, becoming more aggressive; judging their moment. Grim-Uk stepped forward towards Caius, haughty and empty-eyed like he had no soul. He had an evil glint in his red-tainted drug-induced eyes as he switched on his translator.

'My mother died taking all the drugs to conceive my brother Himm-Uk, Caius, and you killed him. My only brother.' Grim-Uk stepped forward out of the shadows, judging his moment, and this was it. Red veins stood out in his eyes as his long sharp teeth chattered in excitement, drooling saliva. 'And you destroyed my pet, my patron. But Bael will return and take your soul. Now I will have my revenge!'

He retrieved the Book of Borossus from a large case and found the page with the incantation, saliva dropping onto the book. His black bloodshot eyes found the passage as Lucia looked on in horror and screamed. 'Caius, kill him, do not let him speak!'

But it was too late.

'*Aifnídio thánato Caius,*' spoke Grim-Uk, his long sharp teeth chattering with excitement. 'Now I will avenge my brother Himm-Uk's death.' Grim-Uk raised his laser pistol as did his loyal Narzuk SS, ready for the kill.

Caius froze. His limbs would not move. His heart pounded as he searched for a solution as the drug crazed red-eyed Narzuks closed in chanting, 'Bael will be avenged.'

Then Caius managed to move his head slowly. He could see the Sigil of the Archangel Michael on his arm and said a silent prayer: *the four Holy words imprinted into his memory by his patron—the four holy words etched into his holy sword that glow silver and blue.*

'Michael! Saday! Athanatos! Sabaoth!'

Time seemed to stop. A gateway opened, and he was surrounded by a blue angelic light, blinding and brilliant.

Grim-Uk and the Narzuk's fired repeatedly at the celestial light, but the blasts were deflected away, scorching and setting fire to a section of the bridge. Caius was now surrounded by a blue fire, *and there was someone else with him.* The Narzuk's shielded their eyes from the light, afraid of what they saw, terror-stricken to the bone.

Grim-Uk retreated in horror at what he saw before him. The entity looked at him with fierce blue eyes, surrounded by blue flames, the Angel who stood before the Throne of God himself, the Captain of God's armies, the Guardian of the Seven Holy Swords of which Caius carries one. The one who thrust Satan and his angels from Heaven now looked fierce and malevolent, and then Grim-Uk knew that he was doomed, as he tried in vain to summon his demon, touching the black macabre figurine around his neck and calling out the name of his god. But his patron Bael could not help him now, for he cowered in the darkness beyond, afraid of the entity that stood before his loyal disciple Grim-Uk, for the God of Caius was stronger.

Much stronger.

The bridge crew looked on in terror at Prince Michael as the bridge descended into chaos, crew running this way and that trying to escape his presence. Then he was gone.

Erg-Ik, the deck officer, put up his hand, but he was ignored. Erg-Ik stood up, 'Marshal, I'm getting some strange readings. I think there is another device in the power plant!' He looked at his screen. A schematic of the power plant was displayed; there is a blinking red light.

'I thought you disabled it!'

'I did sir, this is another one!'

Zurg-Uk's black eyes nearly popped out of his head, as he rushed to Erg-Ik's console. 'Can you disable it from here?'

'No sir, it seems to have some sort of shield!'

Marshal Zurg-Uk pointed at Caius and his party.

'Seize them, seize them! Disable the device in the power plant!' his eyes were wide with panic. But it was too late.

CHAPTER 41

NARZUK TREACHERY

Guards moved to seize Jennifer and Gill, but Jennifer retrieved some holy water and threw it over the approaching Narzuk SS guards, who also had black effigies around their necks. They screamed in pain as their skin blistered and burned.

Grimbald looked nervously at Zurg-Uk, then at Caius, all humour gone from his face. They had been tricked.

But he had his backup plan.

The jumped-up marshal had been his enemy from day one. Now it was time to end it. Time for a new order. He glanced at Grim-Uk, who nodded.

'Detach the central breeding chamber!' Grim-Uk ordered. Above them, a large section of the ship three miles wide separated from the mothership and glided away into the distance, gradually losing height.

Caius whispered to Vinnie under his breath, 'ten seconds.'

There was a deathly silence on the bridge as Erg-Ik tried in desperation to disable the device, his panel flashing red.

In the power plant, alien technicians frantically turned off the device's shield and managed to open it. They saw large red numbers counting down.

Five.

Four.

Three.

Two.

One.

They vaporised as the device detonated causing an explosion, destroying the main power plant for the ship. There was a massive grinding noise as the ship lost power and lurched 45 degrees. The bridge shook, throwing everyone onto the floor as the Sumeri deck officers rushed around the navigation consoles, trying to control the ship.

'Emergency power initiated!' shouted Erg-Ik. But he knew it was too late. The gargantuan ship simply did not have enough power to hold itself up in the sky.

'Divert all power to thrusters and emergency transport!' shouted the marshal trying to save his crew, but he knew that for the ship it was too late.

'Evacuate the ship!' he screamed.

It started losing height.

Panic ensued.

Grimbald and Marshal Zurg-Uk looked around in shock and anger. Jennifer kicked Grimbald in the balls. He fell to his knees clutching his groin, tears in his eyes. Vanessa hesitated but then did the same, losing all composure as Grimbald collapsed to the floor, writhing in agony.

Jennifer stood over him, gloating.

'Take that, you Nazi bastard!'

Gill punched him semi-conscious. 'That's for kidnapping and torturing us, you evil bastard!' Then her eyes blazed red as her talons ripped off his clothes and tear deep gashes into his flesh.

But Grimbald still lived.

Vanessa smiles in satisfaction. Cassian grew larger, fangs emerged from his open mouth, black wings sprang from his back, his hands became claws, and his eyes were red.

'I am Nergal, God of the Dead! I will avenge my dead vampire friends!

'Lucia and Caius, run now!' Cassian's deep guttural voice echoed around the bridge.

Lucia looked pleadingly at her master.

'Cassian?'

'Run! Run for your lives!' he commanded.

Cassian, with lightning reflexes, drew his sword and dispatched the alien Narzuks. His claws sliced through two Narzuk SS officers whose frantic laser blasts bounced off him, turning his eyes an angry red.

'To the escape pods!' ordered Zurg-Uk over the smoke, noise, and confusion.

Caius hesitated. Did he have time to kill Grimbald?

And Grim-Uk?

But then Jennifer and Lucia called him. His wife and lover. 'Save us, Caius! Save us!' Caius turned his head to look at Grimbald, and Grim-Uk, surrounded by loyal Narzuk SS, weapons drawn.

Grimbald was crying tears of agony.

'Grimbald. Grim-Uk. You were lucky today. Next time we meet I will kill you both!' Caius then turned his back and barged forward as Narzuk SS scattered and fled as he led his team out of the bridge. As Grimbald's attention was diverted, a human slave girl lunged forward and stabs him in the leg, smiling in revenge.

'Take that you bastard!'

Vinnie found his knife, but it was too late to take revenge on Grim-Uk as he joined his companions. 'I will kill you next time Grim-Uk!' he shouted as he followed his companions through the fire, smoke and chaos.

Smoke billowed from the left corridor, so they took a right. The mothership creaked and groaned, as its innards had been torn out. Like a wounded animal, the ship lurched again, throwing them off their feet.

Caius shouted to Lucia above the noise and confusion.

'This way I think.' Lucia nodded.

'Why don't we use the escape pods? There, look!' he shouted. They scrambled two at a time into an escape pod. A panel flashed asking for a code.

'Fuck this, it needs a code!' shouted Caius. They rushed out of the pods. Miraculously they found a working transporter and piled in. Lucia entered their RV sector number - Sector 51.

'Hurry!' shouted Caius. Lucia poked her head out of the transporter looking for her master, but there was no sign. 'Cassian!' she screamed.

On the bridge, there was chaos. Grimbald and Marshal Zurg-Uk headed for the escape pods on the edge of the bridge. Just before Grimbald climbed into his pod, Marshal Zurg-Uk grabs his arm.

'This is all your fault Grimbald, you should have killed the human Caius when you had the chance. You will pay for this. Just because you are the emperor's pet, that will not save you!'

In the confusion Grim-Uk saw his moment, retrieved the assassin's knife hidden in his boot, and walked silently up behind Marshal Zurg-Uk as he was about to climb into his escape pod in the wall of the bridge. In a lightning stroke, he stabbed him in the lower back. Zurg-Uk gasped in surprise as Grim-Uk, using his unnatural strength, brought the razor-sharp knife right up to his neck, green blood oozing from the dying marshal's back.

'You have failed the Empire, Zurg-Uk. And the price is death!' Grim-Uk whispered into his ear, as Zurg-Uk collapsed to the floor of the bridge, mouth and eyes open in a look of shock, but not moving. Grim-Uk smiled at Grimbald as he climbed into his escape pod. Grimbald, in a sea of pain, returned the smile and saluted his ally.

Everything was going to plan.

CHAPTER 42

ESCAPE

Grimbald entered a code into a panel, buckled himself inside the pod and a Narzuk trooper sealed the hatch. Grimbald then pressed a red button to fire the escape pods rockets. It's rockets fired as it launched upwards: blackness for a few seconds then it escaped the stricken mothership, soaring up into the blue Californian sky.

The lift door juddered, the lights went out, then came back on again. Nothing happened. 'Are we stuck?' asked Vinnie. Then the elevator shut, and moved at tremendous speed as they were thrown to one side of the wall of the lift, glued to the wall by centrifugal force. No inertial dampers thought Caius, lucky it works at all.

Eventually, the elevator stopped abruptly. Caius, Vinnie, Lucia, Jennifer, and Gill stumbled out, battered and bruised, to the corridor outside the landing area: Sector 51. They met up with out-of-breath Mike and Sebastian.

They all stumbled as the ship lurched at 45 degrees, sending them flying to the floor. Smoke billowed down the corridor; fires were raging everywhere as Caius checked that everyone was there. Cassian was missing. He looked at Lucia. She shook her head.

'He has sacrificed himself so we could escape. Felix and Gabriel are missing too.'

A single tear rolled down her cheek. Caius looked at her.

'We need to get off this ship.'

Handsome Mike grabbed Caius's arm.

'My device didn't work! The shielding device!'

'It wasn't supposed to, mate,' replied Vinnie.

'Subterfuge, they were meant to find it,' Caius replied.

Sebastian hugged Caius.

'Caius, Vinnie, you have your wives. God be praised!' Then he did a double take as he looked at Gill.

'Looks like we're descending,' Caius was anxious.

Sebastian steadied himself. 'Looks like a crash landing.'

Caius looked around him at their equipment.

'How many parachutes do we have?'

Vinnie shouted above the creaking, grinding and explosions happening all around them. He coughed on the smoke.

'Only four.'

Caius spotted an alien fighter launch bay 200 feet away to their right, and a single black fighter craft. Vinnie looked at him. Caius shook his head, 'We have no pilots. By the time we have worked out how to fly it, we'll be dead.' Vinnie nodded in agreement.

Lucia recovered herself.

'I can take Gill and Jennifer but we need to get lower, I cannot fly this high up!'

'We're about 15,000 feet, we need to jump. Now!' Sebastian shouted as he retrieved their hidden parachutes.

Caius and Vinnie hesitated as they looked at their wives, knowing they were not trained to use a parachute.

'We need to go now!' urged Sebastian.

Caius looked at Gill and Jennifer.

'We are going to jump now Lucia, you jump after us. We need to get out before the ship blows with us on it!' Caius insisted.

'I can glide,' Lucia responded and nodded, 'but it will be difficult.'

Caius looked at Jennifer, then at Gill.

'Lucia here will look after you. See you on the ground!'

Jennifer wrapped her arms around Caius and kissed him on the lips, not letting go, as he reluctantly donned his parachute. He had no helmet and no suit, they were lost earlier in the chaos.

Caius crossed himself as Lucia unlocked the exit door and they were hit by a howling gale of wind. Smoke from numerous fires poured in. They coughed and spluttered as the SAS men stood on the edge, then exited the spaceship and jumped into oblivion, hands and feet splayed to slow their descent. Caius moved his arms and legs and steered himself away from the mothership. The smoke lasted just for a few seconds, then he was in clean air.

Caius glanced back at the massive crippled ship, which was breaking apart. Huge pieces were falling off, heading towards the ocean. He looked at one piece from the lower section of the ship as it fell 200 yards from him. He could feel the force as it passed. He slowed himself and steered himself away from the object.

Caius pulled the cord at 5,000 feet, as the fallen piece of ship was several hundred feet below him, then it hit the ocean with a huge splash, causing large waves. He looked up at the mothership, hoping to see Lucia and Jennifer on their way down.

Nothing.

He should have waited for them—*regret fills his heart as he descends.*

Vinnie was 50 feet away. He could see blue sky and, in the distance, the smoking ruins of Los Angeles. Alien fighter craft and escape pods were fleeing the doomed black monolithic mothership like ants fleeing a damaged nest, flying in a confused manner. But they were being met by a squadron of F22s, Gatling guns blazing a trail of fire. More pieces of the groaning mothership were falling off, as it lurched this way and that.

Still no sign of Lucia and Jennifer.

Had he failed?

Was it a lost mission?

He should have strapped Jennifer to him somehow.

Had he made a bad decision?

CHAPTER 43

A MOMENT OF TREPIDATION

Caius has an empty feeling in his stomach as he guides his chute to avoid the falling debris, and it plummets into the sea. The mothership must be at 4000 feet now and in danger of breaking up. An alien fighter craft flies dangerously close to them but then shoots off towards the open ocean, ignoring them.

Back on the crumbling mothership, Lucia is shouting to Jennifer and Gill. Jennifer is confused,

'How can you fly? We will die!'

Gill replies, 'Lucia is a vampire like me.'

'Let me show you,' shouts Lucia above the noise and smoke.

Lucia transforms into a vampire, her red eyes blaze, her incisor teeth turn into fangs, with black leathery wings. Jennifer falls to the floor and faints.

'Well, that makes it easy.' Lucia grabs Jennifer and looks at Gill.

'You need to carry me too, my wings haven't grown yet!' shouts Gill.

They wrap the arms of Jennifer around Lucia, who binds them to her with some para-cord and Bergen straps.

'Gill, you next,' says Lucia as she prepares more Bergen straps.

As they stand on the howling ledge of the mothership, the ship lurches again, and Gill falls off into the air, falling, falling. Although she is a vampire, Gill's half-formed wings flutter and slow her down, but she cannot fly. She cries for help as her small wings struggle to support her.

'Lucia—help me!'

Lucia dives off the ledge with Jennifer strapped to her tight, her head pointing downwards so she can streamline her way through the air to the flailing Gill. Lucia gets closer, 10 feet, five feet, one foot, then finally reaches her. Gill wraps her arms around Lucia's waist, but Lucia cannot hold her because her arms are now black leathery wings.

Lucia looks back up, hoping to see Cassian.

Nothing. Where is her master?

Her eagle eyes then look down to find Caius, the man warrior God, her passion, her ancient love, but there is too much smoke. Where is he?

'Caius, Peter da Bulletproof, I need you now!' she cries as she carries an unconscious Jennifer, his wife. If only Jennifer knew that she and Caius were once man and wife, in ancient times, in Rome, in happier times, now they are brought together again, by the unseen forces of fate, to help mankind. She will tell Jennifer when the time is right. The look in her eyes told her she remembered her from long ago—that ancient longing.

Can a vampire, a demon, feel love?

Caius has two wives now. Both love him—*could it work?*

All these thoughts and fears rush through her as tears fall from her red eyes. Jennifer opens her eyes to see a tearful red-eyed demon looking at her. She is panic-stricken, and shivers in the cool air, as she clings to Lucia's cold demonic body, her eyes wide-eyed in terror as she looks up at the mothership groaning in its death throes. Jennifer, her heart pounding with adrenaline, has a moment of trepidation. Will she see her husband again? Peter, Caius, the Warrior God. They have come this far only to be split apart.

AGAIN.

Lucia holds her tighter. They have come this far, she doesn't want to lose her now. Besides, she is growing closer to Jennifer, she feels excited that she is reunited with her lover from long ago, she holds her tighter, as her black wings carry her through the air. And she is reunited with her long-lost love, Caxus, now Caius—that is, if they can avoid the crumbling mothership, bits of which plummet past them as she flies.

The massive alien mothership is losing height and is rapidly heading towards Earth; flames, and smoke pouring from various parts of the ship. It is heading for the sea just off Los Angeles. The suction from the downdraft is pulling Lucia towards the ship. She is fighting against it with all her strength, but she is weakening.

Lucia looks at Gill the vampire, who is clinging on for dear life.

'Gill I cannot carry you both. You must fly, become da demon!'

CHAPTER 44

LONG BEACH

Gill looked at Lucia with trepidation, unsure. Her life depended on her becoming the demon. Then something changed in Gill: her eyes become red, and her wings grew, and she laughed a demonic laugh.

'I am immortal!' she cried.

Caius and Vinnie guided their chutes over the ocean towards the smoking ruins of Los Angeles. Caius was glad it was an MC-6 steerable parachute, great manoeuvrability, and a lower rate of descent compared to the MC-1 system which he had used before in his HALO drops.

In the distance, they could see the golden sand of Long Beach. Caius was relieved to see dry land as they aimed for the golden strip of sand a few miles distant. Below them they could see the white tops of large waves caused by the huge pieces of wreckage falling from the ship. He could hear the faint crash of the waves, even from a few miles out as they landed crashing onto the beach. They dropped lower and could taste salty moisture in the air; they were now only 500 feet above the ocean as they saw another massive wave pass below them and reach halfway up the beach.

'Fifty feet high,' thought Caius. Then he realized the danger. He signalled to Vinnie and Sebastian, pointing a finger to go higher up the beach. Vinnie nodded as they pulled on their cords to steer them further up the beach. Four hundred feet, and they were still over the ocean. Caius tasted the salty air. Three hundred feet, as another white-crested wave passed below them, Caius frantically pointed up the beach, as they were falling fast. He could feel the spray on his face as they guided their parachutes over the waves and up the beach, and then landed softly on the golden white sand, out of breath.

They took their parachute gear off and looked around them, relieved to have made it. Alien craft were flying backward and forward over the beach, and over Los Angeles—ignoring them, no doubt in a panic, thought Caius. Then all of the craft, en masse like starlings, headed out towards the ailing mothership as the squadron of F22s, attacked what was left of the alien monster-ship.

Caius looked up to see any sign of Jennifer and Lucia. There was a tiny speck in the distance, but he could not make out what it was. Then Caius looked around him. Vinnie, Sebastian.

'Sebastian, where's Mike, I thought he was with you?'

Sebastian looked sad, then shook his head.

'I lost him on the way down. He got hit by a piece of the mothership. He didn't make it.' Sebastian crossed himself.

They hung their heads in silent thought, Caius felt the warm sun on his head, and a cool breeze brushed his face. Soon he would be reunited with his wife again, and go back to their home in Wales, and spend time with the kids. Everything would be alright again, and he could return to a normal life. Vinnie joined him.

'Any sign of Lucia and Gill?'

Caius was silent as he gazed up at the speck in the sky, using his hand to shield his eyes from the sun. The speck got larger by the second. His eagle vision focused on the speck, expecting to see Lucia and Jennifer.

But it wasn't. As he focused, he could make out the shape of a winged vampire.

But it wasn't Lucia.

The vampire flew closer and landed on the beach. It was a fierce-looking female vampire with large black wings. Vinnie ran over to the red-eyed entity and stood before her, unsure.

'Gill, Gill—it's your Vinnie! Is that you?'

The vampire looked at Vinnie as if she only half recognized him. A distant memory came to the surface. Yes, this was her husband, when she was human. His name? Her eyes changed back to their normal brown color, and her wings shrank, as she, at last, recognised her husband. 'Vinnie!' They both threw their arms around one another.

As Caius gazed into the distance with his binoculars, he could see hundreds of fighters streaming out of the stricken mothership in a panic, going in all directions. Then another squadron of F22s flew noisily overhead at supersonic speed, heading for the mothership and the panic-stricken alien fighter craft, making a furious defence of the fatally wounded mothership. He watched as they encountered the alien fighters, who fired their laser weapons, but the F22 shields were holding this time.

The F22 pilots retaliated, firing their recently fitted Sirius Gatling guns with good effect. Though not destroying the black fighters, they were spinning out of control and crashing into the sea a few hundred yards out. Caius watched as an F22 was hit by multiple fighters, shields failing, and the pilot ejected just as the F22 exploded in a ball of flames. The fighting moved closer to the mothership, which seemed to fill most of the horizon, and was losing height.

Caius was walking around in circles, 'Where are Jenny and Lucia?' thinking about his wife and lover. 'Lucia couldn't hold me any longer, she had to let me go,' Gill replied despondently.

'I turned at the last minute,' whispered Gill now almost recovered from the ordeal. 'That was the last time I saw Lucia and Jennifer.'

Caius was downcast. He was so close, then he lost her at the last minute. He should have stayed with her, on the ship.

Vinnie put his arm around his best friend, 'Don't give up, Caius.'

A tear fell from Caius' eye as he looked up at the sky, hoping upon hope that Jennifer and Lucia would appear. Big, tough, hard man, warrior Caius, and he was crying.

'There is every chance she can make it Caius, Lucia can make it,' reassured Gill the vampire.

They all crowded around Caius, trying to console him.

He had failed. He had failed her. He had not rescued her as he had promised. He had broken his promise. He would go home to Wales empty-handed—*what would he tell his children?*

Caius got on his knees and looked up at the sky,

'I'm sorry Jennifer. I have failed, pleased forgive me, my love!'

A dark cloud blocked out the sun as he knelt on the beach, disconsolate, black thoughts running through his mind. His chin rested on his chest. At that moment he prayed. He prayed to the Holy Archangel Michael, his patron, to take away his darkness, and fill him with hope. Find his wife Jennifer, and Lucia, his secret vampire love. His wife Jennifer, and Lucia, both wives, but from a different moment in time. One from the present, and one from Roman times.

The image of Michael came into his mind, a powerful and beautiful long-haired angel in blue robes carrying a long sword, which shone like the sun. For a moment he had the impression of heaven, the place where Michael dwelt, where time itself did not exist, but past, present, and future were one and the same. A place of golden temples, paths encrusted with gold, diamonds and emeralds, lush green meadows, magnificent waterfalls and the constant singing of the angelic choir - the music of heaven. Peace filled his heart as he prayed.

CHAPTER 45

REUNITED

Then he saw his friends looking up into the sky. The clouds parted, and the sun came out again. There was hope as his eagle eyes scoured the sky.

Looking.

Hoping.

In the distance, he could make out a speck in the sky. An object—no, two objects; two people. 'I see something. Two people.'

Caius focused his vision, then smiled.

'Correction. One vampire, one human. Yes, it's them, it's Lucia and Jennifer!' Caius jumped for joy as they came closer, coming into view, Lucia's large vampire wings flapping. Jennifer was hanging on for dear life as they landed on the beach, both collapsing onto the sand exhausted. Lucia did not move for a second, then stirred.

They ran over to them, as Jennifer stood up, her jacket falling open, as Caius hugged her and kissed her. 'You made it!'

'We both made it,' she replied.

'You OK?'

'Yes, fine, a bit out of breath. Come here, soldier boy.' They embraced and kissed and both shed tears.

'I never gave up hope. I knew I would find you! Even if I had to search to the ends of the Earth,' said Caius, tears falling from his eyes.

Then they held each other and just sobbed. Lucia got on her feet, now fully recovered, shaking her long black silky hair, speckled with sand, and looking at Caius with her blue smouldering eyes, as she donned a cloak to shield her from the sun. The sun beamed down on them as they stood on the beach, grateful they had escaped from the horror of the mothership.

Grateful to be reunited.

Jennifer looked at Lucia, her long dark hair, her beautiful face, alive and shining eyes, and curvy body; half in admiration, and half-curious as she looked at the magnetic Lucia, then at Caius, searching for a sign.

'Strange company you keep. She's pretty, isn't she?'

'Without Lucia, we would not have found you. Not in a million years.' The sun went behind a cloud, and Lucia took off her hood.

'Thank you, Lucia. For saving me.' She felt attracted to Lucia, as though they shared a common bond. 'We have met before haven't we?' Lucia nodded. Jennifer smiled with genuine warmth, and hugged Lucia. Jennifer felt a strange bond with Lucia as she felt her long black hair brush her face, and Lucia kissed her on the cheek. Jennifer had a vision of sunny days in a Roman villa as she kissed a naked and blue-eyed, black-haired beauty—*it was Lucia!* Lucia was her lover from long ago.

Then they both turned, arms around each other's waist, and smiled at Caius, admiring the God Warrior: husband and lover.

'Magnificent, isn't he?' said Jennifer, admiring Caius's body.

'He's a foot taller now,' said Lucia.

'I wonder what else has grown?' said Jennifer as she looked at Lucia and they both giggled. Then they both cuddled again as Jennifer played with the earlobe of Lucia. Then she kissed Lucia on the cheek, then on her blood-red lips. Lucia's attraction was magnetic as Lucia ran her hands through Jennifer's long brown hair. Jennifer kissed Lucia on her lips again and then walked over to Caius. She blushed as she looked at Lucia, then she hugged Caius tighter, not letting him go. When she was with Lucia in Roman times, Lucia's husband was there too. Somehow he reminded her of Peter Caius. Was there a connection? It was all a bit vague, then she wondered about Vanessa, on the ship.

'Where's the First Lady? I admired her,' said Jennifer.

Caius shook his head, 'She's got a lot of balls, the First Lady.'

Lucia shook her head in sadness.

'I lost her in the confusion.' But Lucia was more concerned for her master. 'Any sign of Cassian? He is not in my vision. Where is my master?' she cried.

Caius and Vinnie shook their heads. Caius touched Lucia's shoulder

Jennifer's eyes darted at him, but she was not jealous. There was a connection between Lucia and the mighty Caius, her husband.

'I think he sacrificed himself so we could get away. A gesture of great love for you Lucia,' said Caius.

'I think he has found redemption,' Sebastian tried to comfort her.

'Cassian was very human for a vampire,' reassured Caius.

'Thank you. He would have liked that,' smiled Lucia. Now it was Lucia's turn to feel downcast, a tear falling from her eye.

'Thank you for finding me, Lucia, and helping my husband. I'm sure your friend Cassian, will turn up,' comforted Jennifer. And this time it was Jennifer's turn to look Lucia in the eye, knowing she was a lover from long ago. She kissed Lucia on the cheek, then she hugged her as her hand moved down to Lucia's perfectly shaped round bottom. Lucia responded, pouting her blood red lips, then held her tight and gently kissed Jennifer on the lips, their tongues meeting.

'Your name was Juliana,' whispered Lucia. Jennifer nodded and smiled, fragments of memory swimming through her mind. 'My husband was Caxus. Remember? Caxus has been reborn in Caius. We are both bound to be him Jennifer! He is our husband!' as she kissed her on the lips, then they both looked at Caius, tears in their eyes.

Caius smiled, he was glad Lucia and Jennifer seemed to be getting on so well. It could have been awkward, and then he realized that Lucia and Jennifer were the women in his dream, from long ago, when he was a Roman. Come together through time and space, to be reunited once more. Both wives, both lovers.

Everything seemed to be working out. His eyes felt wet as he looked at them and his heart felt only love.

CHAPTER 46

WALL OF DANGER

They sit on the beach, filthy and exhausted from their ordeal, as they watch the alien mothership in the distance, filling the horizon, going through its death throes, the monstrous black monolith slowly losing height, then faster, as it moves inexorably toward the ocean. The ship is almost at 90 degrees now, lurching, struggling to stay upright. It seems to move in slow motion, filling their vision.

A small crowd of refugees gather on the beach; dirty, dressed in rags, but with a look of relief on their faces, as they watch the spectacle.

'Why did you disable the first device?' asks Vinnie.

'Vinnie, I had a prescient vision,' Caius replied.

'A what?' asked Vinnie.

'I saw a brief glimpse into the future. I knew you would be captured on the bridge. If both devices had gone off, we would all have perished. The first device was a red herring; they were supposed to find it.'

'Lucky escape then,' said Vinnie as he relaxed on the beach.

Caius had a feeling of anxiety as he looked at the ship, but couldn't quite work out what it was. They were safely out of the ship, sure, but…

'How far out do you think that ship is?'

'Maybe 15, 20 miles—what of it?' asks a weary Sebastian.

Caius continues, although he is not exactly sure why he is asking the question.

'How big do you think it is?'

'Maybe one hundred miles across.'

'Pretty fucking huge,' adds Vinnie.

A frightening thought is entering Caius's mind.

'How deep is the sea, do you think?'

Sebastian replies nonchalantly, not sure where this is heading.

'Maybe 2000 metres.'

'Probably make a bit of a splash, won't it? When it lands, that is.'

'In the water,' Vinnie added, now fully aware of their danger.

'Er, yes,' said Sebastian. 'Oh shit,' as he crossed himself. Sebastian and the others realise what Caius is getting at.

'Oh shit.' Caius stands up.

Vinnie grabs the radio. 'I'm going to signal base for pickup.'

'Sebastian, have you got any binoculars?' Caius asks frantically— even his eagle eyes need more focus.

Caius adjusts the binoculars to focus on the flaming mothership as it crash-lands into the sea. A third of it disappears underwater, the rest of it clearly visible, displacing the ocean as it strikes the water.

He can see the sea rise several inches as he sees a solid wall of water heading away from the crashed ship - at a tremendous speed. Not a regular shaped wave, but literally a wall of water. Caius is alarmed, his adrenaline pumping.

'We need to run!'

'What's the hurry? I was going to relax on the beach for a bit,' says Jennifer as she lies on the sand sunning herself, next to Lucia who is covered in a cloak. They are holding hands smiling at one another.

'Run!

'Why? The spaceship is miles away!' asks Jennifer innocently.

'Tsunami! Heading our way!'

'Oh shit!' his wife replies.

They run towards the city. They seem to take forever getting off the beach. Jennifer trips over and Caius half-carries her, then she trips over again. 'Get on my back!' he cries as Jennifer jumps on his back and Caius sprints away, faster than an Olympic 100-metre champion. Lucia is too exhausted to fly and runs with the rest of them. As Caius gets off the beach, he is relieved to hear the sound of a helicopter in the distance.

He can hear something else, too. He has a memory of his childhood holidays in Cornwall, playing on the beach, and the sound of big Atlantic breakers, foaming white. But no, it is more of a roaring sound, like a freight train approaching. He turns around but Lucia is already looking. All the water is receding from the shoreline at a frightening rate, exposing the ocean floor. A wind catches his face as he gazes out to the impending danger.

Caius knows the tsunami is near.

Caius can see an enormous wall of water, 100 feet high, approaching Los Angeles. It is maybe a mile or two out, but traveling at a tremendous speed. His keen eyes can actually see sparks like lightning coming off the top of the wave. Caius and Lucia quickly overtake the others as they dash for safety. Vinnie is pointing as he dashes off to what Caius knows will be the RV for the helicopter.

They don't have much time.

Even the mighty Caius cannot not survive a towering tsunami which will have the crushing force of 100 tons when it hits. Their only hope is to create some distance between it and them.

Caius catches up with Vinnie.

'Pattinson Park, just up ahead!' shouts Vinnie, pointing the way.

'Run!' urges Caius.

Caius's heart pounds in his chest as they run for their lives, a roaring sound following behind them. An alien patrol takes off, leaving some clones behind, looking stranded and lost.

They run across the Pacific Coast Highway, through a small industrial park, and onto the green grass of Pattinson Park. They can feel the ground vibrate as they hear a roaring sound behind them. The helicopter, a four-bladed, twin-engine Black Hawk, is waiting for them. The pilot waves frantically for them to hurry. It is Kojak.

'Hurry laddy!'

As they board the Black Hawk, the roaring becomes much louder, and they can a feel a rush of air like an approaching storm. As the helicopter takes off, they hear an enormous roar as the tsunami hits the beach at tremendous speed. It does not break, but keeps going—a solid wall of water now 50 feet high. The giant wave rushes towards them—*a towering wave of destruction.*

'We need height, Kojak!' shouts Caius above the roar of the impending wave. Kojak flies vertically for 50 feet but then struggles to gain height as there is a tremendous wind from the tsunami, and struggles with the controls, swearing and bitching as he pulls the elevator lever—*they watch the wall of foam-topped water speeding towards them.*

CHAPTER 47

HEROES

Kojak regained control, said a short prayer of thanks, crossed himself, and they gained valuable height, as the wave roared below them, like an express train.

Just below the helicopter, they could feel the spray from the wave and could taste salt water in their mouths through the open window. As Kojak gained more height, they headed out of Long Beach city towards the mountains on the edge of the city. They looked out of the window at the destruction below.

Below them, the city was flooded as the wave continued its inexorable path, killing and drowning aliens, clones and humans alike, destroying houses, flooding, and damaging offices, warehouses. People clambered onto the tops of houses and climbed the stairs of derelict buildings to escape the onrushing flood.

The Black Hawk was now out of the city and over some low hills, La Habra Heights. A few houses and ranch-style properties were dotted here and there, as they flew over a golf course which overlooked the city. The helicopter lost height and landed on the grass in front of the clubhouse of the Hacienda Golf Club.

It looked dark and derelict as they got out of the helicopter, onto the overgrown grass. Caius turned to the pilot, 'Good job Kojak, that's the best bit of flying I have ever seen. Very close call!'

'Glad to see you made it Pete, laddy!'

'Any activity?' asked Caius.

'Nay, skies are clear now, no alien activity. Good job—the X-37D we used is in a shite state,' replied a relieved Kojak. Then he joined the others on the lawn and lit a cigarette for a well-earned smoke. Lucia stood alone and dejected, looking up at the sky, pining for her master as Gill, the newly bloodied vampire stood beside her, trying to comfort her.

They were met by a beaming President Wilson, General Scott and Professor Picard. President Wilson shook the hand of Caius.

'Caius, you did it, you actually did it…well done. You are all heroes!' Then the president shook everybody's hand, in turn, congratulating them.

'You didn't have to flood the city, but well done!' General Scott added jokingly as he shook Caius's hand. Caius was reticent and silent, as he remembered the bad blood between them, just nodding.

'Jolly good show—outstanding, in fact!' General Scott added as Caius turned away.

President Wilson walked up to Caius, anxious. 'The First Lady, my wife, Vanessa, did you see her?' he asked, a mixture of hope and anguish in his eyes.

'Yes, we saw her, but I am sorry…we lost her on the way out.'

President Wilson hung his head dejectedly as Caius put his hand on his shoulder, feeling genuine affection for the man.

'Sir, she was very brave, she displayed great strength of character. You should be proud. You should have seen her.'

'Vanessa…Vanessa,' repeated the president, head drooped, trying to cling on to hope.

'She kicked Grimbald in the balls,' Caius smiled trying to cheer him up.

'Good,' said the president. 'Did you kill him?'

'I'm sorry I didn't get a chance sir, he escaped. But one day we will meet again. Then I will kill him.' And that bastard Grim-Uk he thought.

'At least you found your wife, Caius, I am happy for you.' The president was sincere as he looked Caius in the eye.

'To be honest, I thought I had lost my wife too, then I prayed to my patron Michael, and she came back. Do not lose hope, Mr. President. There is always hope, that's what makes us human.'

Jennifer stood on her tiptoes and kissed Caius on the lips.

'I love you. My hero!'

'I love you, too. I've had enough action for a while. Let's get back home and see the kids,' Caius said in a deep yet gentle voice.

General Scott approached Caius.

'You can get back home after the debrief son. Just to bring you up to date. In the UK several, major cities have been re-captured, including Birmingham. The western part of the UK, including Wales, is probably safe, son. The eastern sector, including London, is still occupied by the bastard aliens. Again, well done, son.'

Caius turned away with Jennifer, then for a second, Caius's and

Lucia's eyes met. A moment in time that said a thousand words, a moment of understanding, as if to say, we will meet again Caxus.

Lucia then saw the professor and hugged him. 'Uncle Louis, you're safe!' she smiled, a tear in her eye.

'Cassian?' asked the professor. Lucia shook her head. Then she looked up, as she sensed something, something familiar. She stood transfixed, searching the sky, hoping beyond hope.

In the sky, she saw a speck, and wings, large black leathery wings, a dark shape appeared Cassian! The winged red-eyed demon appeared carrying the First Lady. They all looked up at the pair. As they landed, the president rushed forward and hugged his wife with great joy.

'I thought I had lost you!'

Lucia hugged Cassian, as he returned to his normal appearance, and gave one of his rare smiles.

'Lucia, my child.'

The professor approached Cassian. 'The Book?' Cassian shook his head. They approached Caius in anxious anticipation. 'Caius, did you manage to retrieve the Book of Borossus?' the professor asked hopefully.

'No. The bastard Grim-Uk has it,' answered Caius, through gritted teeth. 'This war is far from over,' he added, knowing the magical hold that Grim-Uk now had over him. Professor Picard and Cassian looked dejected.

'But at least we are reunited again, so let's count our blessings,' smiled Caius, trying to brighten the mood.

'Oui, mon ami you are right,' smiled the professor as Lucia put her arm around the aging genius. Picard, with perfect timing, retrieved a bottle of champagne from his bag—Dom Perignon—which Caius took and opened with his thumb, took a swig then handed it round.

'Excellent year,' Vinnie joked.

Lucia took a swig and burped, then laughed, happy to be reunited with her master and uncle. Cassian gave one of his rare smiles.

Jennifer joined Caius. 'I like Lucia, she's nice,' said Jennifer taking another swig of the champagne. 'I need to see her again.' Caius smiled and nodded. It might just work out.

CHAPTER 48

GOING HOME

From their vantage point, they have a good view of the now-flooded L.A. basin and the ocean beyond. They all turn and look at the massive crippled alien craft in the far distance as it explodes again and sinks beneath the ocean, only partially submerged, the shattered remains of the 100-mile bulk of the black mothership in ruins.

They watch as a beautiful sunset lights the sky. They stand and look at the spectacle. More explosions erupt from the ship, orange flames pepper the massive bulk. Caius puts his arm around Jennifer as they watch the mothership and the sunset, feeling a sense of peace and happiness. Now he has his Jennifer back.

He looks at his wife again, and notices she looks a bit grey around the edges. After all, she has been through a terrifying experience, anyone would look off-colour after what she had been through, he reasons.

General Scott gets everyone's attention. 'We had better move, we're going to nuke the mothership, just to be sure.'

'Better safe than sorry,' adds Caius.

They evacuate the hilltop in two helicopters. Caius and his team all crash out, in various states of exhaustion. Caius looks at Vinnie, knowing his thoughts.

'England?' Vinnie nods as he hugs Gill. Caius knows his family is in danger. Their homeland needs saving too, but is it too late?

Elated, tired, but happy Caius cannot relax, he is restless as the helicopter moves off. Jennifer sits next to him and holds his hand.

'I have some news,' whispered Jennifer.

'What is it?' asks Caius. Then, he notices the bump in her tummy.

'You're pregnant!' Caius jumps for joy and hits his head on the helicopter roof, Vinnie laughs as Caius rubs his head, and then hugs his wife, but as he holds her in his arms, he notices her neck, the skin looks a little green. Jennifer is pregnant, yes.

But is it his, and is it human?

EPILOGUE

CATALINA ISLAND BEACH

General Grimbald emerges from his crashed escape pod; half-drowned, bruised, exhausted and in a terrible mood as he crawls through the clear blue water onto the white sandy beach. The fading sunset reflects on his face as he crawls out of the sea onto the sand out of the surf, coughing up water and trying to catch his breath. His uniform is torn to tatters as he collapses onto the beach. His leg is bleeding from the slave girl's stab wound, the sea running red.

As he lies there he sees green alien eggs wash up onto the beach. He can see movement in some of the eggs, which are semi-transparent. He watches as one of the green eggs breaks apart, and a half-human, half-alien baby emerges. It has light green skin and blue eyes, and a large head. It turns its head towards him, blinks, then lets out an ear-shattering scream. Grimbald shudders as it starts to crawl towards him on the beach, thinking Grimbald is its mother. As it gets to him, he pushes the baby away in disgust, and it starts to cry.

Thousands of Breeding Pods from the mothership start washing up onto the beach. Some human females, survivors of the breeding pods, stagger out of the pods and collapse onto the beach. The rejected baby crawls towards a blond woman lying half-naked, recovering on the beach. As it gets to her, it starts to suck the nipple of her breast. Milk oozes from her breasts as it sucks. She does not push the baby away but puts it on her chest, stroking its head as its eyes look at her.

Grimbald finds a medical kit from the escape pod and puts alcohol and bandages on his leg, and on his bleeding gashes. He staggers as he stands, a wild look in his eye as he shakes his fist into the air like a deranged dictator.

'You think you've won, Scott? You think you've won?'

Some 50 miles away, in the direction of the semi-sunken black mothership, is a brilliant flash of light. Grimbald shields his eyes from the sun-like nuclear blast and mushroom cloud forming in the distance.

TO BE CONTINUED IN BOOK FOUR...

REVIEW

If you like my book, I would be eternally grateful if you could give a ☺ review

The story will be continued in – REVENGE (Battle for London) DOMINION First Blood Series Book Four

Sign up on my website for new book releases, free books, stories behind the books, competitions, news and gossip, sample chapters

My blog www.richardmannblog.com

Follow me and Like my Facebook Page:
facebook.com/richardgmann.author

Facebook Group: Richard Mann Author Sci-Fi Group

Follow me on Twitter: @richardgmann

Search Dominion First Blood on Google and Youtube

See the Movie Trailer for this book

Please share – Your friends will love it!

https://tinyurl.com/y8nksqmw

https://www.youtube.com/watch?v=4Tn7mt9dgcQ

Search Dominion First Blood Hero, Vendetta or Caius on Google and Youtube

ACKNOWLEDGEMENTS

My thanks go to Les for her help with the book cover. To my patient wife Brenda as I spend endless hours in front of the computer on my book as she gently asks, when will it be finished? And thanks to Led Zeppelin for keeping me sane during the long hours at my keyboard.

APPENDICES

Cockney Slang	Rhymes with	Meaning
Cream Crackered	Knackered	Very tired
Pen and ink	Stink	Stinks
Tom and Dick	Sick	Sick
Bees Knees	Business	Effective
Adam and Eve it	Believe it	Would you believe it?
Boat race	Face	Face
Tom Tit	Shit	Going for a shit
Alan Whickers	Knickers	Women's Knickers

VAMPIRI COMMAND STRUCTURE

COUNT CASSIAN OF ROMANIA *1

LUCIA

VISCOUNT VINICIUS OF BRAZIL *2

LORD ASWERNE OF THE PHILIPPINES *2

BARON TITAS OF GERMANY *1

LADY VESILIA OF ENGLAND *1

RAJA VAMDEVI OF INDIA *3

SIR ELIJAH OF AUSTRALIA *1

BARON ALEXANDER OF RUSSIA *2

*Notes number of legions commanded

Sumeri Alien Command Structure

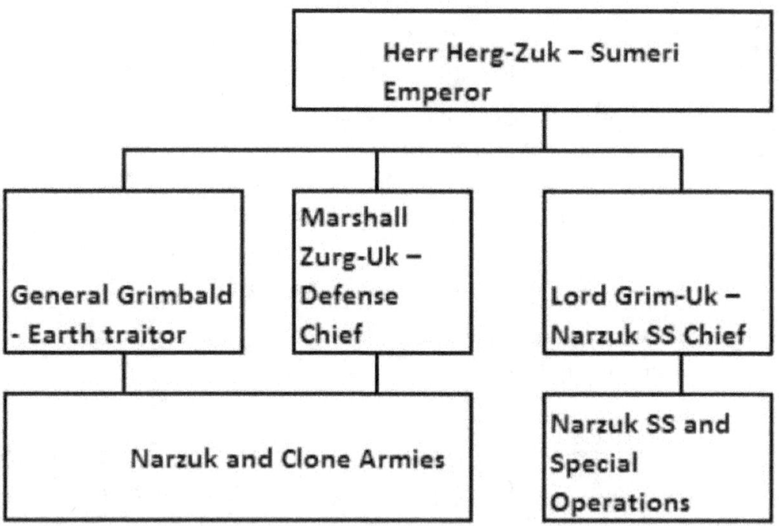

AFTERWORD

Although this is a work of fiction *(and I hope you enjoyed it very much)*, there are elements of truth running behind it.

Did aliens visit ancient Sumeria *(Modern day Iraq)* at the earliest point of human civilization?

Many scientists are astounded at how Sumerians progressed so quickly from mud-hut living fisher folk to temple building mathematicians. Did aliens experiment with early human DNA to kick-start the human race? *(There are many books on this subject).*

'The 'Sumeri' aliens in the story arrived and 'integrated' at that time with the Sumerian civilization 6,000 years ago.

Do aliens really exist?

Truth is sometimes stranger than fiction. As technology advances and more and more 'M-Class' planets *(those capable of sustaining life)* are found every year, then the probability increases that aliens do exist. In fact, there are 140 billion habitable planets in our galaxy alone.

William Hill, the bookmaker, has slashed the odds of a UK prime minister or US president announcing aliens are visiting the planet from 1000/1 to just 25/1. It follows Hillary Clinton's pledge to "get to the bottom" of "unexplained aerial phenomena" if she is elected president. She also vowed to send a "task force" to Area 51 in Nevada where alien craft are rumored to be hidden away. *(Is that why she lost to Trump ?* ☺ *).*

In 2011, the FBI declassified decades' worth of secret government documents. These documents contain thousands of reports of UFO sightings and alien activity. These include Mass UFO sightings, personal abductions, and government cover-ups. Most interesting among these were reports of huge triangular shaped objects flying over Belgium airspace in 1990.

There were hundreds of reports of these objects, frequently described as enormous and triangular in shape – known as "The Belgian Wave," which lasted for two years. Air Force Supersonic F-16 jets chased these strange objects, which were simultaneously tracked by both airborne and ground radars. The Belgian Government cooperated fully with civilian UFO investigators, an action without precedent in the history of government involvement in this field. These triangular objects have been reported all around the world, along with increased activity in abductions and mysterious alien implants. The question is, are these man-made craft developed from secret alien technology, or real UFO's?

Hypnotic regression of abductees seems to suggest an alien agenda of aliens experimenting on humans to breed half-human, half-alien hybrids. Any official question to governments about these mysterious sightings and events is normally met by a stony silence or a grumpy rebuff.

What becomes clear is that sightings by a few people can be 'covered up' by government disinformation etc., but sightings by hundreds or thousands of people, including photographic evidence, *(as has happened),* cannot be covered up. I came across another story, so spine-chilling that I will not repeat it here, but it suggests the war against aliens has already started.

The circumstantial evidence for alien activity appears to be overwhelming. The US Government has been collecting evidence from UFO crash sites around the world for decades. I understand why they keep it a secret, and I think they should keep it a secret, for obvious reasons.

Should SETI *(the organization set up to Search for Extra-terrestrial Intelligence)* be actually trying to contact aliens in the first place? Should we stop sending signals to outer space trying to contact aliens? Professor Stephen Hawking seems to think so *(and I would agree with him).* In the movie Battleship, SETI sends a signal to outer space which is picked up aliens who then proceed to invade our planet.

Oops.

Indeed, our current technology has not advanced to the point where we could defend ourselves against an alien invasion. But, how would humankind fare in an alien invasion? What do the experts say? Military strategists from the Air Command and Staff College in the United States have a multitude of plans if aliens did invade. They have war-gamed every scenario imaginable.

Unfortunately, most of that is classified as Top Secret information, i.e., they want to keep quiet about it. Reading between the lines, I do not think humankind comes out of it very well.

Is it likely aliens would ever invade our world? The conclusion by scientists was that an invasion was likely. Why?

1. They want to breed with us because they can no longer reproduce themselves (like the Sumeri aliens) - or

2. They want Earth's resources - Water, metals, forests, and biology - or

3. They want the Earth as a new home for themselves *(and presumably, evict us, Earthlings)*. This could be because their own planet is no longer habitable. *(Maybe they polluted the atmosphere or destroyed their own with wars - does that ring a bell?)*

There is a United Nations office called the UN Office of Outer Space Affairs Committee based in Vienna, which is charged with the responsibility of making first contact with aliens with its own ambassador, Simonetta Di Pippo. His office is tasked with sending a message in all major languages to the extra-terrestrial visitors. The universal language of mathematics would also be used by transmitting prime numbers to the aliens.

Aliens are likely to be highly intelligent and advanced scientifically. In the 1930's Germany was the most advanced technological country in the world, developing their war machinery in secret collaboration with the Russians, deep inside Soviet Russia. The allies were oblivious to this – and as we know, the allies did not know about the advanced German technology until it was too late.

In the second World War, the British and French were completely overwhelmed by the technically superior German war machine – leading to the evacuation at Dunkirk. The allies were completely unprepared and complacent about the Nazi threat – leading to a scramble to re-arm, which the British did with amazing speed and innovation.

Would aliens be friendly? We only have to learn the lesson of Nazi Germany to understand that the answer would be no. There appears to be no relationship between technological advancement and moral or ethical behavior. The aliens in this book are the embodiment of evil, just as the Nazis were in WWII, and they were desperate enough to adopt the Nazi ideology. Is that a warning to us?

In a war against aliens, the whole world of politics and alliances would be thrown on its head. Former enemies would become allies, NATO soldiers fighting alongside Russian troops - just as it was during the Second World War *(perhaps even sharing a shot of vodka during the fighting)*. Imagine American troops fighting an alien menace alongside the Taliban and Al Qaeda *(unthinkable I know),* because it is not a war of ideology, but of human survival – the future of humankind itself.

Perhaps in a moment of reflection, everyone needs to look beyond his or her own navel, and self-interest, and think about what is best for humankind.

Nevertheless, even if old enemies did join forces - will that be enough? Who will help the human race in its darkest hour?

Look for friends in unlikely places.

Do vampires exist?

Do you know anyone who, when they speak to you, just drains you of energy, with their vindictive and bullying attitude? *(Maybe someone at work)*. Perhaps their physical presence send shockwaves and shivers through your body, making you feel weak and defenseless. To all intents and purposes that is a vampire, because they suck the energy out of you. Some people just feed off the psychic *(and physical)* energy of others.

Do you know someone like this?

Vampirism has existed for thousands of years - cultures such as the Hebrews, Mesopotamians, Ancient Greeks, and Romans had tales of demons and spirits, which are considered precursors to modern vampires. However, in history that is more recent the folklore for the vampires seems to originate almost exclusively from early 18th century southeastern Europe, and the famous tales of Count Dracula in Transylvania.

Another example of truth being stranger than fiction is that the X-37D stealth aircraft mentioned in the story is based on a real experimental space plane - the X-37B. The X-37B design resembles a mini-shuttle and is only 29 feet in length and fifteen feet in width. The unmanned, reusable vehicle logged an unprecedented 675 days in space, but very little is known about this Top-Secret space plane which seems more 'James Bond than a machinery of reality.'

The US military keeps very quiet about the X-37B – but it has been orbiting the earth for the last two years and landed recently at Vandenberg Air Force Base in California.

This fictional story discusses the existence of a worldwide military organization to prepare for, and fight, any alien attack, namely Sirius. This worldwide network may, or may not, exist, but it would certainly be prudent to prepare for an alien invasion and is within the realms of probability. All the 'Sirius' weapons discussed in the story may seem like the stuff of science fiction but in fact, are based on real technology. The X-37B, railgun and laser technology as well as the Adaptiv armor which hides vehicles from infrared, are based on real technology.

Although we would appear to be defenseless against an attack by an alien force, all is not lost, because we humans have something they do not, *we are greater than the sum of our parts*. In great adversity, we find the spirit, the wit, to win our way through - somehow. Remember the Battle of Britain where a handful of Spitfire pilots defeated the might of the Luftwaffe? When our lives are on a knife-edge, humankind finds a way through.

Somehow.

Although this is purely a fictional story it does raise issues about our existence, how we look at the world, our neighbors, and our attitude to how we should treat others that are not like ourselves. Issues of race, ideology, religion, sexual orientation, wealth and class are irrelevant when your own existence is in peril.

More than anything this story is about the friendship between Peter and Vinnie, childhood friends, and the desperate need for peoples of all races, to come together to fight evil, whether the source of that evil is from this planet, or from a different one. This Book is a warning against extreme politics like the Nazi movement foolishly adopted by the alien invaders.

My research on the SAS has revealed their essence, men who have pushed themselves to their limit - beyond physical pain, beyond what is possible for normal humans. Men who can think on their feet, and remain calm under pressure. The Thinking Soldier. The SAS selection process tests their metal, to see if they are made of "The Right Stuff." This is why Peter has an epiphany when Des and Artie ask him how he passed selection. 'I see the truth of it,' is his cryptic reply.

As Winston Churchill famously said, "Sometimes doing your best is not good enough. Sometimes you must do what is required." We as humans must always strive to be the best we can be to fulfill our Destiny.

In some ways, I have been through my own version of SAS selection. Getting up at 4am for 6 years to work on this book as well as doing a full-time job in addition to family responsibilities. I sincerely hope you will look kindly on this book and give me a nice review, and recommend this book to your friends and work colleagues. My ambition is to be a full-time writer so I can write the next exciting installment in the Dominion series!

HISTORICAL FOOTNOTE

Ergal Five is the home of the Sumeri people, the name also given to the people in ancient Sumeria, in what is now called Iraq. Whether the Sumerians got their name from the alien invaders in 5000 BC, is open to debate, but historians, including Professor Picard, have found ample evidence of alien activity at the time of the Sumerian civilization. The astonishing rise, of the Sumerian people from living in mud huts dwelling fisher folk to ziggurat builders *(pyramids)* and the first picture-writing system on tablets *(known as cuneiform)* to mathematics has always astonished researchers and scientists. They made laws, were ruled by kings, and were probably responsible for the invention of the wheel, among other things. Professor Picard was of the strong opinion that the alien Sumeri, were, in fact, the catalyst, that projected these people to great achievements, though they suffered at the hands of the aliens as well.

A million years ago, Ergal Five used to be a thriving civilization of 1 billion people, living in peace and prosperity. Most of the population lived on the continent of Zuk, where the main cities of Erg, Kuk and Hik and the capital Sumer were located. Zuk had a mild Mediterranean-type climate where food production was plentiful with many varieties of fruit and vegetables. They built large cities, temples, farms and huge pleasure palaces. Like many civilizations, they celebrated the seasons and had many festivals, including Akitu á-ki-ti-še-gur10-ku5 "cutting of barley," akiti-šununum "sowing of barley", rêš-šattim "head of the year") was a spring festival in ancient Mesopotamia, originating from the Sumeri people.

The name is from the Sumerian for "barley." There were two festivals that celebrated the start of each of each half of the Sumerian calendar. The sowing of barley in the autumn and the cutting of barley in the spring. In Sumeri religion, it was dedicated to Marduk's victory over Tiamat, their gods. All was abundant and plentiful.

Before clones came along, the social structure was evenly balanced and based on a meritocracy. People who worked hard were rewarded, and the majority of society was generally happy. They had enough to eat and clean water, their homes were comfortable, and there was time for relaxation. There were artists, painters, writers – there was freedom of speech. There were libraries and schools and parks as well as the Zuk factories, which produced all they needed. People were happy, and on the whole, satisfied with their lives.

However, they turned away from nature, and things started to go wrong when the natural environment was not respected. Their technology was advanced, but they chose to rape the forests for building, turning them eventually into deserts. The rivers and seas became polluted from massive factories, pouring chemicals into the rivers and seas which soon became a chemical soup, killing all sea life. The people complained they had no fish to eat.

The inhabitants suffered lung disease due to the polluted air. Lifespan shrank from 150 to 100 years. As the land became more polluted, food shortages became common, and the Sumeri started getting diseases, whereas before there was none. Water was so scarce that only rich people could get hold of it.

The Sumeri people started invading other planets to raid food and water, even though in the past they had friendly relations with other species.

Now - there was war, civil unrest on Sumeri and conflicts with neighboring races on other planets, which were previously friendly. They started becoming infertile, and fewer babies were born. And so the cycle of decline began, with increasingly desperate measures.

Soon, the Sumeri women became mostly infertile *(except for a few who could afford the outrageously expensive, and dangerous, drugs and treatment)* and population growth stopped and went into decline. They hit upon the idea of cloning themselves to re-populate themselves. They built vast factories, producing thousands of clones. Each clone was based on a real person.

ABOUT THE AUTHOR

Richard Mann grew up in being an avid reader of books, even from an early age he loved the literary giants JRR Tolkien, Michael Moorcock, Frank Herbert and Douglas Adams. *(If you like this kind of books you will love Richards books)*. He started writing at 16 and started a book called tales from Mellyms Tarc, with a character called Gluloidic. The dream of becoming a writer faded until a few years ago when he started writing again. During his twenties, he studied business studies and accountancy. During this time, he also studied Shaolin and Wing Chun Kung Fu and even started a school with a friend. He has worked as an accountant, Software developer in the City of London for banks and insurance companies, and is now an author.

His mercurial work is action packed, fast-paced, and guaranteed to keep the reader turning pages to the end. This wholly original book falls within the Sci-Fi Post-Apocalyptic, Superhero genre with elements of thriller and horror. It combines incredible action, hair-raising scares, and big laughs. It will shock the reader into thinking about his own place in the world. Warning: This book may keep the reader up all night!

Richard is a Fellow Member of the Association of Accounting Technicians, Member of the Institute of Analysts and Programmers and a Member of the British Computer Society. He is in his late fifties, married, has two sons and lives in Berkshire.

The best way to keep up with his latest news is to
sign up for his newsletter.

www.RichardMannBlog.com

FEEDBACK TO THE AUTHOR

If there is anything you would like to see in my books, please send me an email.

Give feedback on the book email: richardgmann@yahoo.co.uk

Follow me on Twitter: @richardgmann

Follow me and Like my Facebook Page:
facebook.com/richardgmann.author

Facebook Group: Richard Mann Author Sci-Fi Group

Sign up on my website for my newsletter for book updates, new book releases, stories behind the books, competitions, news, and gossip.
You can easily signup by entering your name and email.

BOOK MOVIE TRAILER

See the Movie Trailer for this book

Please share – Your friends will love it!

https://tinyurl.com/y8nksqmw

https://www.youtube.com/watch?v=4Tn7mt9dgcQ

(or search google for Dominion First Blood).

www.ingramcontent.com/pod-product-compliance
Lightning Source LLC
Chambersburg PA
CBHW070358200726
48294CB00003B/983